Beneath the Hills

... a collection of writings

by Ochil Writers' Group

Volume II

Resonate & Blue

First published by *Resonate & Blue* in 2017
(Imprint of **Tatterdemalion** Blue)
in association with Ochil Writers' Group

Layout by **Tatterdemalion** Blue and Ochil Writers' Group

A CIP catalogue record for this book
is available from the British Library

ISBN 978-0-9933114-5-1

www.tatterdemalionblue.com

Supported by **Scotmid**

Beneath the Hills ...

... a collection of writings

by Ochil Writers' Group

Volume II

Don't tell me the moon is shining;
show me the glint of light on broken glass.

Anton Chekhov

Contents

Foreword

The Ochil Writers' Group was perceived to be a gathering of like-minded people where individuals could find inspiration and the confidence to express their thoughts while also honing their skills and supporting each other.

In time there comes achievement, and in 2011 this came by the way of the publication of the first volume of the group's anthology 'Beneath the Hills'. Much of this achievement was due to the guidance of Tom Murray, the Writer in Residence in Clackmannanshire. His support and belief in the ability of the group and his lasting encouragement enabled the group to take that first step into print. This volume was lauded as an excellent first anthology and it gained 5th place in the Nationwide Group Anthology Competition and received a Certificate of Commendation.

This second volume comes after a gap of some years over which time there have been several changes in the make-up of the group. However, members have striven to maintain the standards already set, and this second volume of 'Beneath the Hills', with its diverse topics, styles and genres, will, I am sure, contain something for everyone to enjoy reading.

The writing is unfussy, the voices clear and unique, filled with a directness which is refreshing, intelligent and heart-warming. This an excellent compilation of poems and stories by local writers, who hopefully will go from strength to strength and receive further recognition.

Caroline Crawford

Edgelands

by Monika E. Mackenzie

"The area is dead - nothing there - no-man's land!" ... this was the general opinion in the town. It was a rusty, red-brown stretch of land, way off, beyond the railway tracks, where people seldom went for any reason other than to dump things.

Even on sunny days it looked bleak, unkempt - a wasteland, though once part of this town. At the far end, one could make out some scrubland with stunted blackthorn bushes, adorned by wind-ribboned plastic bags fluttering in the breeze. The ground for the most part was covered by red slag - legacy of a once proud local brickworks. The only other surviving evidence of its existence was a small, tumble-down gate-house made of red brick, with the door off its hinges, but the grimy window and corrugated metal roof intact. Against its wall on one side grew tall, brightly-coloured Foxgloves, and the area in front was overgrown with the delicate blue flowers of Crane's Bill and feisty yellow dandelions.

It was there that they found her. Two lads, bored, forlorn and quite possibly bunking off school, with a scruffy mongrel at the end of a length of rope, were kicking a dented Pepsi can about.

When the dog started barking, they let it run off, thinking that it had probably spotted a rabbit. For a while, they carried on playing footie but then stopped and turned in the direction from where furious barking could now be heard. Sparky was standing by the open doorway of the disused little gate-house, totally beside himself, when suddenly he went quiet and approached the space where the door should have been.

"Can you hear that?" one of the lads, Joe, said to his friend, pointing towards the small graffiti-covered shelter. They looked at each other in consternation.

"Someone singing!" Archie looked spooked. "Should we have a look?"

They quickly covered the distance of about hundred yards, unsure of what they would find and not feeling entirely courageous.

At that moment, they saw Sparky coming out of the hut, carrying something in his mouth. Immediately, he sat on the ground and began chewing something that was obviously very tasty. Joe tried to call the dog towards him in order to take whatever it was off him.

"It's all right!" they heard someone call out, "it's only a biscuit."

The two of them scanned the area around them but could spot no-one. They looked at each other, perplexed, and then - without further ado - took the few steps to the hut's entrance. Neither of them was quite sure what or who they would be confronted with.

"You go first, Joe", Archie said and shoved him before they both lost their nerve.

What Joe clapped eyes on after he was catapulted into the interior of this place left him speechless - but only for a second.

"The Bag Lady???"

"I am Evelyn", she said, quite matter-of-factly.

She was sitting on a stool, well … more of an old slatted apple box really, one leg stretched out in front of her. Beside her on the floor was an old mattress, covered with a clean piece of rug.

"Is this where you live?" Archie sounded incredulous.

"Yes, I came across it by chance", she smiled. "It's lovely out here in the summer."

"Folk in the town have often wondered where you disappear to when you have done walking the streets during the day", Joe said to her. He was a little embarrassed. He also wondered what there could possibly be liked about this dump of an area.

"People are not interested in someone like me. I am surprised they even gave me a thought."

Archie and Joe looked at each other, unsure of what to say.

2

Then they looked at her leg. After a few awkward moments, Archie asked: "What happened to you? Your leg doesn't look so good."

The Bag Lady gave them a brief smile: "I think I have broken my ankle. It must have been my guardian angel who brought you two here this morning. I am so glad your dog found me!"

Bending down, Joe patted Sparky and said: "Clever boy!" and then turned towards his friend: "Have you got your mobile with you, Archie? We need to get an ambulance. It's far too far for her to hobble to the main road, even with our help."

Archie grinned and nodded: "I got it back yesterday. My Mum had confiscated it because I was running up bills."

While they were waiting for the ambulance, the two boys tried to find out more about Evelyn's life and why she did not live in a hostel, at least.

"This place is full of wonders", she told them. "If you walk over towards that burn, where the large patch of rye grass is growing, you will understand more about it. Go quietly and very slowly and you will come across something very beautiful."

They did as she had suggested, and when they finally reached the spot they looked around, wondering what she had been talking about. Then, Joe felt Archie's hand gripping his arm. He looked at Archie and then at what he was pointing at: below them, among the long tufts of rye grass was a small, brown-speckled bird, crouching down on a nest and giving them a startled look. His face broke into a smile.

When they went back to the hut, Evelyn took one look at their faces and said: "Corn Bunting. They are ground breeders. Ten eggs in the nest. They should be hatching soon and I'll miss it if they keep me in hospital. I'll have to explain to them that they can't do that!"

Archie thought for a while and then volunteered: "Perhaps, they'll let you out with a stookie!" He didn't sound too convinced, though.

"Something I have been meaning to ask you for the last half

hour." Joe's face had a puzzled expression which caused her to raise her eyebrows.

"Yes? What is it?"

"Aren't you afraid out here all by yourself? I mean, it's dangerous for a woman."

"Most of the people who come here are young 'ns like you and people who walk their dogs and play 'fetch' with them. I have a good nose for those I can trust. And if I am not sure I keep out of sight."

She tried to get up and gave a little cry - her ankle was clearly giving her a lot of pain. From afar, they could hear the sound of an ambulance. She turned towards them urgently: "Could I ask you something? You come here quite often, don't you - I mean, when school is out ..." - she winked at them. "Could you possibly look after my flowers? There is a tin in the shed. You could go over to the burn for water and take care of my lovely garden." She gestured towards the self-sown Violas, the Foxgloves, blue-flowered wild Geraniums and Dandelions.

Joe and Archie were a little unsure as to whether she was, perhaps, joking. When they lifted their heads to look at her they realized that she was utterly serious. They began to understand how important this place was to her.

"We will. When it is dry, we will come down here with Sparky - he likes to run around and be daft. When it is raining we won't - obviously." Archie heaved a sigh. When was the last time anyone had trusted him enough to ask for a favour? He suddenly felt good.

When the ambulance finally got there - it could, of course, not cross the railway tracks as Archie and he did - Joe helped to get her onto a wheel chair. Then he bent towards her and said: "We'll visit you in hospital. If you'd like us to, that is."

Evelyn looked up at him and gave him a smile, then said: "I don't know what would have happened if your Sparky hadn't found me! I am so relieved and I thank both of you for coming to my rescue."

Joe and Archie were quite embarrassed and looked at their

shoes - before blurting out simultaneously: "Weeelll, it was all thanks to Sparky really ... and for the fact that we skipped school today."

Evelyn laughed, then winked at them: "I won't tell, I promise. And yes, please, do visit me in hospital. You can tell me about yourself and we can get to know each other better ... if you want to."

At that point, the paramedics moved forward and proceeded with loading Evelyn onto the ambulance. The two youngsters waved, before the driver secured the ambulance's back door and made ready to drive towards the town, away from this no-man's land.

The Mop and the Janitor

by Mary Perry

The mop and the janitor
fell in love
the moment that they met.
He took her by her slim white pole
and covered her dreadlocks with sweat.
"Let me take you to the Assembly Hall",
said he, leading her on the floor.
This made her feel sensations
she had never felt before.

"Oh Janitor, dear, my love divine,
although my pole is not real pine,
it's made of considerably durable stuff.
Oh Darling, I really can't get enough.

I can bend to your whim
And sway to your sway.
Oh Janitor Darling,
I love you this way.

Oh Darling, I love it
When my dreadlocks are hanging
Close to your armpits
When I hear your heart banging.
At lunch, let us go
To your battered chaise-longue
And lie down together,
Making music and song."

Coincidences

by Denise Macdonald

Like many things in life, Miss Bunch was deceptive. Not quite what she seemed to be. To most people, she was a small, inclining to plump middle-aged lady; a useful sort. Just who we need, was frequently said by those who had tiresome or tedious tasks to perform. Miss Bunch will do it! And Miss Bunch always did. Indeed, she enjoyed creating order out of chaos. She liked things to be neat and tidy. Square everything off, pile even thoughts tidily, and then, well - then, there was space for dreams.

Miss Bunch was a fairy godmother. Underneath her sensible navy-blue or grey clothes was another outfit entirely. The only hint of this other self was the red shoes she occasionally wore. She was not a real magical fairy godmother, of course, although that was where the idea had come from. Reading fairy tales, as a young girl, she had never wanted to be the princess; she knew it wouldn't do. After all, princesses were never practical with braids and freckles. Princesses could not toss pancakes or run into the wind; they had to act with decorum. Miss Bunch had no truck with decorum when she was a child, but time had foisted it on her. So, on the outside she was tidy, neat, geometric in her precision, well-camouflaged. On the inside where the almost magic was, there she could still run into the wind.

You might wonder what kind of magic Miss Bunch could do? She arranged coincidences. It really was just a matter of adding one and one, and knowing just which one to add. Of course, it was a coincidence that Sadie Green happened to be having tea with Miss Bunch on the very day her ex-boyfriend was fixing the gate. Such a silly argument, so easily resolved over tea and scones. It was a coincidence when Miss Bunch happened along just when Mrs Pettigrew needed a baby-sitter, in order to make preparations for an unexpected dinner for some visiting Japanese businessmen her husband had invited to their home, never imagining for a moment they might accept. Another coincidence was that Miss Bunch had a book on Japanese flower arranging in her bag just borrowed from the library and how surprising that she spoke Japanese! Miss Bunch delighted in being a fairy godmother; she asked for nothing in return. Sorting things out neatly and tidily was enough. And because she asked for nothing ... well ...

Miss Bunch was a little tired. Her desk was piled with last-minute reports all marked 'urgent', but it was her day for lunch out. So here she was, sitting on the second bench along in the park. The morning had been busy and the afternoon looked like it would be, too. She took out the sandwich from her bag and bit into it thoughtfully, wondering for a moment if the wind she liked to run into in her mind could be persuaded to blow through the office. Absently, she pulled at the crust and then threw it towards a pigeon. Soon there were several pigeons.

"Oi, what do you think you are doing?" shouted a voice.

"Feeding the pigeons!" The voice had startled her into an answer. An overalled figure stood with a spade in his hand, eyeing her over the flowerbeds - one of the park gardeners.

"You know what will happen if you keep that up?" he demanded.

"No?" Miss Bunch glanced over at the sign-post near the park gates, which bristled with notices offering dire warning of penalties for different behaviours. She could not recall anything about pigeons.

"We'll have fat pigeons!" he laughed. For the very first time in her life Miss Bunch did not know what to say. Luckily, he broke the awkward silence. "Well, these dandelions won't weed themselves!"

"Ah, I am sure you are right", she gathered her things together, "I have to go; lunch break, you know."

"Well, most people get an hour. You have only been sitting there ten minutes." He startled them both with this remark.

"Good luck with the dandelions", she offered and walked away. He watched her go. A tidy useful sort, but those red shoes? He had nieces who were shoe-daft; he knew about shoes! He glanced over at the bench and noticed a small notebook on the ground. She must have dropped it. He turned to shout after her but she had gone. Putting down the spade, he went and picked it up; maybe it was not her notebook? It had a glittery fairy on the front and extra stars stuck to it. Perhaps, one of the children who used the play-area had dropped it? He flicked through it looking for a name. Rosie Bunch. The name made him smile. There seemed to be list at the front - a shopping list, perhaps? Maybe he could take the notebook to the shop and hand it in there?

He looked at the list. Alice meet Mark at 6pm, in the library. Where is Miss Withington's hat? He frowned. It seemed to be a list of arranging meetings and finding hats. A strange list, but at least he knew where she would be at 6pm; he could casually hand the notebook to her there. Besides, he had not been to the library for a long time - high time he visited it; his neighbour, Miss Beaton, worked there. She had said that very morning that they would be putting on an exhibition and a pity a big strong man like him couldn't turn up and help. He picked up the spade. It had taken him a couple of weeks to speak to Rosie - nice to know her name; she always sat on that bench on Tuesdays. It had been those red shoes that had drawn his attention, made him think of that film. Whistling 'Somewhere over the Rainbow', he went back to tackle the stubborn dandelions.

Rosie had mislaid her notebook. Never mind - it would turn up eventually! She knew what she had to do today: she had agreed to help with the exhibition at the library and had arranged to take up some things that had belonged to her great-grandmother, a Suffragette. Alice, a university student who lodged with her neighbour, had agreed to help. Perfect. She knew that Mark would be there that evening. He was studying to be a doctor - such a nice boy but so intense and a real worry to his grandmother, who was a particular friend of hers

9

and another contributor to the exhibition. It would be an easy thing to arrange an accidental meeting - no trouble at all really, which was more than could be said for that hat.

He had gone home and spruced himself up, put on his best casual shirt, worried over a tie and then decided not to look too formal. He was early. He good-eveninged Miss Beaton and then retreated to the furthest bookcase, romantic fiction. He picked up a book and idly leafed through it and then, his attention caught, started to read with an air of disbelief. Miss Beaton eyed him over the top of her glasses and smiled rather severely. She didn't know any other way to smile - it went with the job, she believed. Librarians should be severe as custodians of all human knowledge; they had to take their work seriously. She glanced at the clock - 5.55pm - and smiled as the door swung open and in walked Mark with a large box. He ledged it awkwardly on the desk and glanced back to see the door open again and Rosie and a slender blonde girl walking in, both struggling over a large box. He dumped his box quickly and moved to help. Rosie beamed as the young people stared at each other. Miss Beaton smiled at Rosie and then glanced at Tom, who was staring over the top of the book at Rosie. She called to him: "Tom, could you come and lend a hand? Ah, Rosie, you have met Tom Gardener, haven't you? He's a neighbour of mine and a wonderful gardener!"

Tom hastily put down the book and walked to the desk.

"Yes, I have seen Rosie in the park on Tuesdays. It is nice to meet you properly and, I think, you left this behind this afternoon?" He handed her the small notebook.

"Isn't that nice?" Miss Beaton said. "So, now everyone knows each other. If you could take those boxes through to the lecture room you could help set up. I shall be serving refreshments in half an hour", she added. They smiled at her, a small slender figure with steel-grey braids wound tightly around her head, and faded blue eyes that seemed to see everything over her old-fashioned half-moon glasses. She was the backbone of the information in the small town, seemed to know everyone and everything; really, she was a walking book - they all said so. Those people who said things. Miss Beaton sighed. What did they know, those people who said things? No-one knew that she was really a fairy godmother. What did she do? She arranged meetings. She watched them walk through the heavy swing door and then reached under the counter and took out a large leather bound book. She opened it and stared down at her list smiling as she put a big tick next to Rosie Bunch and Tom Gardener and then frowned over the next entry, it really should not be on her list at all. Where was Miss Withington's hat?

The Alchemical Magician

by Mary S. McLuskey

The streets in this part of town were narrow and foreboding and no-one walked here at night by choice. The buildings seemed to tower above, leaning inwards so that their tops appeared to touch at the sky's edge. Edward Keene walked swiftly but not too fast so that he did not attract attention. He wanted to be done with his task before midnight so he could return to the warmth and safety of his own private quarters. Around him in the street, Edward could see no other but still he sensed their presence.

In the distance a dog howled at the night as a misty fog began to descend upon the streets, giving the already frightening place a more sinister feel. Edward involuntarily pulled his cloak closer to his neck and renewed his determination to get to his destination before the night was out. He walked with a graceful ease that set him apart from other men, for Edward was a dancer and becoming quite famous now that the play he was in had been given Royal approval. People flocked to see the play and the daily papers raved about Edward's performances. People marvelled at his skill and artistry and his strength. It was said that no other dancer, not even the greats of the past, could match Edward's presence on stage.

When he rounded the corner Edward spotted the doorway he was seeking; a plain dark green door that he knew led to a very different world than that which it faced. As he approached the door Edward raised his cane and knocked three rapid knocks and when it opened he took a deep breath and stepped through the entrance. A world of magic and wonder awaited him. Gone were the drab and dreary streets, no more could he feel the burden of the night; no longer did he feel tired and afraid. He unclipped his cloak and with a flourish draped it over his arm before removing his hat and placing both items on the small table just inside the door that he had become familiar with over his many visits.

As he strode forward Edward began to relax and he accepted the offer of a refreshing drink from the silver tray that a pretty waitress was proffering in his direction. Music floated through the air reaching his ears and as if by magic, his feet began to move with the rhythm pulling him further into this secret world. Beyond a curtained door way, dancers twirled and jumped across the floor, acrobats in bright costumes swung on ropes and swings dragging paper ribbons of many colours behind them as they crossed the roof space from one precarious perch to another. Edward smiled and waved to his fellow dancers and allowed himself to be drawn into the thick of the crowd, laughing and dancing as he went.

He reached the far side of the room far more quickly than he had wanted and he felt a hint of sadness touch his heart as he moved away from the party towards his real destination. Before him was yet another door, one through which he had passed many times and one which he had grown to both fear and hate in equal measure. In the centre of the door was a large knob, which rested among ornately carved shapes of animals and men that swirled around the doors centre. Edward watched the carvings as they began to move, slowly at first then faster and faster, like a train running around a circular track. Mesmerised, Edward felt himself being drawn into the swirling circles of animals and men and just as he felt he was going to fall over, he was suddenly in the familiar surrounds of the gothic corridor that lead to the place he so longed to be.

The froth and fun of the dancers at the party were long forgotten now as he made his way carefully along the velvet-swathed corridor. Now and then, metal nuzzles protruded from recesses in the walls where suits of armour stood protecting nothing in particular. Their gun metal finish provided a contrast to the green velvet curtains that hung from the walls and the plush carpet which softened his tread as he walked gracefully along the length of the room. Edward had no fear, only trepidation; what if the thing he sought was no longer available? How would he live without that which he had come to love and desire so much? What if the Magician was unwilling to provide what he needed?

The warmth of the room, its soft colours and gentle feel did nothing to betray what lay beyond the final door. As Edward approached this door he was again struck by its simplicity. There were no elaborate carvings, no polished door knobs, not even a lick of paint. This door was made of solid oak and showed little sign of wear; indeed the oak looked as fresh as if it had just been cut from the tree. Edward did not need to knock or to push at the door as he took his next steps, because as he stood in front of this green door it simply opened to reveal nothing but blackness. The feeling of fear from the first time he had stepped over this threshold into the unknown washed over Edward and was gone in almost the same instant. He knew now there was nothing to fear, but that first time he had taken a leap of faith that had proven so far to be of the best decisions he had ever made.

Now standing inside the blackness, he was aware of the soft touch of what he knew to be ivy creeping around his legs and up over his body, clasping him in an embrace so strong and yet so gentle that he had no trouble in giving himself over to the plant's will. He was lifted high in the air, way up to where there was light and to where she waited for him. Watching his ascent, Edward wondered what she might look like today. On previous visits she had changed her hair colour, her age, even the colour of her skin. She had been tall on one occasion and on another tiny, like a little elf. She often wore wings of gossamer but he had never seen her fly and as to her eyes, no matter how he tried Edward could not find words to describe their beauty. She was every woman and she was his. She loved him, she had said so and she gave him a precious gift; immortality and with it eternal youth.

Edward stepped onto the ivy-clad platform as his bonds gently released him onto firmer ground. He stood tall and felt invigorated, as if the ivy itself had fed him some magic elixir. He looked for her, but she was not sitting on the throne that took pride of place in this heavenly setting. Instead he could see that she was standing off to one side, her back to him and she was hiding something from him. Edward strode forward, wanting to see what she was hiding and to his astonishment saw a boy that looked exactly like himself when he was about seventeen, the very age he had been when he had first come to this place. She smiled at Edward and held out her hand, beckoning him forward. Slowly and a little unsteadily, he moved towards her. She was the most beautiful he had ever seen her and the boy seemed to glow with a radiant energy that made him, too, look unbelievably beautiful.

She spoke and for the first time, Edward heard her voice. "It is time", she said and took hold of his hand whilst simultaneously letting the boy's hand go.

Her voice was like an echo and her touch deathly cold. Edward felt his strength flowing away from him as he watched the boy grow older before his eyes. The boy took on more and more of his own features as he himself grew weaker and weaker. She spoke again: "It is his turn. He is now the Alchemical Magician and he will rule the world as he sees fit. Edward, your dancing days are over."

She turned to watch as Edward sank to the ground an old man, like Methuselah. The boy, now man, stepped forward; he reached down to Edward and lifted his face toward him: "I have waited 969 years to take your place. You have danced for the last time and I must find my role in this world."

The man-boy turned and looked at the woman: "She will keep you and care for you as she does for us all. Perhaps, one day in a thousand years we will meet again."

Edward watched as the ivy lifted the man-boy away from where he stood taking him to the green door, the velvet corridor and the world beyond. From somewhere in the recesses of his mind he thought the scene familiar, but he dismissed the idea as he realised that before him was a small crowd of old men, each one looking older than the next.

"Oh", he said. "I think I understand."

Just then, the woman reappeared, this time dressed in more sober clothing but still as beautiful. "Come", she said, "join the family and tell us all of your stories for we have not had a new member for so very, very long."

Quest

by Monika E. Mackenzie

Hesitant, this brave first step
into life's winding labyrinth
of well-worn paths
and those less travelled.

Not unlike Theseus, I set out on this quest
past pitfalls and great tribulations;
past mirrors found at every bend
in this precipitous landscape,
reminding me of who and what I am.

Now and then I'm encountering
a sunny vista softening my resolve,
but very swiftly learn to push aside
that which impedes my progress.

High passes and tight passages attempt
to test my metal, enabling me to make
sound choices that'll ultimately
assist me in my search.

Each phase through which I walk
is two-fold in its purpose:
detaching me from what I was and knew,
then guiding me to find that other self.

And in this altered state
my heart, too, gently changes
as I approach the dreaded centre
that holds my inner fears, my darker side,
intent to slay my Minotaur.

Infinite Resurrection

by Gary Smith

On a perpetual nightmare
(an undying season of torturous brain weather) ...

The hope of an escape that would annihilate the mind for good,
walked the plank - much farther than that point where earth
and universe merge as time without end
and I did emerge as what I had been before -
a dreamer with but a vision to defend;
a dreamer, with but fantasies on which to depend.
But as keenly as a virus infiltrating pores,
all that had been declared godly entered my heart;
as keenly as the chauvinist instigating chores,
all that was supposed satanic entered my heart.
Only astonished, I fell to knees on shredded memories.
Only astonished, I searched the sky for emotions to apply.
Much more than astonished, my sickness deep inside, for once,
did not confide; merely doubled up then died.

As I stood by a cavernous hill, where at the age of 30 years I was born,
I questioned why it took so long for my foetal mind to form,
an exquisite feeling sat down next to me
and proclaimed a notion of intent -
that all life would live inside of me,
if I would just allow a magic, heaven sent.
"But faith in the untouchable holds no part of me!" I did reply.
That feeling looked toward myself
with a portrait of perplexing insanity and I knew,
right there and then, that I could become the secret five percent
I held in awe throughout all my tragedies but never spent.

That those years that came before, all the evil would be no more,
the black in me would go below and burn in hell forevermore.

So I left man's sacrilege behind and did descend that lonely place;
as I walked toward new life, heavenly beauty appeared by my side,
a distant music did touch me somewhere never touched before;
questions did arise but I just let them fall...
I turned to look and she looked back at me,
eyes that only purity could believe.
We walked on and on towards eternity,
knowing that uncertainty is life
and inside life the only surety is mortality.
We walked on and on, past much suffering and pain ...
There were riots, executions,
theatres of decadence and ever-lasting inquisitions,
ships were sinking; men were killing,
dams were bursting and blood distilling.

The horrors of man eventually became a distant squall
The blisters on our feet – nothing to our call
All creation stood aside as we followed on and on.
For many moons we walked,
until a blissful, lifetime satisfying dawn.
And then came the point we stood to listen
and became conscious of an understanding
there and then we made an eternal connection ...
and the mystery of life revealed itself:
Infinite Resurrection.

"Perfect ..."

by Melissa Macdonald

We all make mistakes, and maybe this was mine. Only I won't feel guilty - there isn't time for that.

I suppose I am lucky really - how often does someone get to choose the cause of death? I am hoping you will see it as considerate that I didn't send him after just anyone - this took careful planning.

It is 20:05 ... He is due any minute. *Perfect.*

I was careful, I burnt the gloves and the sandwich bags; I watched them melt into a black syrup outside.

Now before me - the perfect scene - my bed, messy, just as they left it. The police will find her copper strays littering my side; they were the first sign I had an invader in my so-called perfect life. Three sets of prints will be found; by now two of them will be a thousand miles away - mid-flight to a conference - a good alibi but not good enough. By the time this twisted corpse is found it will be too cold to determine exactly what came first: the flight or the murder.

In my letter, I specified it was to be made to look like break-in, the window smashed but nothing stolen, nothing but the gun. It had to look amateurish - after all, my husband has a lot of secrets it seems, but I can't imagine he has ever killed anyone before ... a scruffy cover-up is what is needed. Their seemingly perfect alibi will be all too convenient.

When the window smashed I was a million miles away; it jolted me back to reality. I knew he was there, I heard him. Feet steadily creaking towards the bedroom.

My last act on this earth - I pulled my wedding ring off my finger and threw it in the direction of the bed. I closed my eyes. In my mind, I played out exactly what was to be suspected. I pictured finding them together; oh, how dramatic that would have been! First throwing the ring, hysterical with rage and confusion - then launching myself in the direction of that fiery serpent, who poisoned my perfect existence with her expensive floral stench ... out of protection and desperation he would - in that moment - choose her.

My thought stopped. **Dead**. An immediate warmth pulsed from my chest. Darkness. *Perfect*. And then nothing, a nothing so soothing to the numbness I had felt for so many months.

My Mother always told me the best revenge was to have a good life. I *had* a good life.

And I made sure theirs would never be the same again.

Leighton ...

by Mary Perry

... the village my mother took me to every Summer, probably from the time I was out of rompers. We always stayed with my Auntie Rose and Uncle Charlie.

Their house, Leighton Cottage, was a chocolate-box idyll - black and white, thatch-roofed, with diamond-leaded windows. In the front garden was a Monkey Puzzle tree, and while a marvel to visitors and children alike, it did become a disadvantage by blocking the sun from entering the house.

The back garden was my delight - I remember from the age of five playing with my cousins and helping myself to gooseberries, blackcurrants, wild strawberries and ... oh! Getting a stick of rhubarb to dip into some sherbet. My Auntie Rose had fruit trees, too, like plum, damson and greengage. It was the job of my older cousins to collect these.

Running through the garden on the furthest edge was a lovely little stream - gentle enough to paddle in and generous enough for sticklebacks to swim. One Thursday, Mum, me and the Fisher kids went to Shrewsbury to get some rabbits, and while we were in the market we saw, on the next floor, some fishing nets, so we bought ourselves one each.

The next day, armed with our new fishing gear and jam jars from the kitchen, we headed to the stream and netted a number of innocent little fish. After plopping two or three into our jars, we proudly walked back to show our trophies. Uncle Charlie was in when we got back and asked: "Do you think those stickleback look happy in those jars?" Well, none of us had thought about the fishes' welfare. "If you keep them too long in those jars they won't be able to breathe. They won't have anything to eat either", said one of my cousins.

We intrepid fishers felt a bit shame-faced by now so returned the sticklebacks to their natural habitat.

Auntie Jessie, Rose and my mother started to prepare Jugged Hare and encouraged us kids to collect broad beans and carrots. We shelled the beans and washed the carrots, but we weren't allowed to chop them; it didn't stop us from chopping one with our teeth, though.

Great excitement! The local school children were breaking up for one week. This meant that the Perrys would be able to join us on our regular jaunt to Leighton Park. To get there, we just needed to stroll four hundred yards. Then, after passing by the post office-cum-village shop to buy some sweets, and for some water from the village pump, we crossed the road, climbed over the fence and were in the park.

And what a beautiful place it was - the trees offered a veritable play park. There were Chestnut trees looking ready to go to the ball in their beautiful green dresses. We just loved flopping on lower ribs, then swinging back and forth. The Oak and the Ash offered other pursuits, like climbing, making rope swings and playing 'Tarzan' or, if the Perrys and Margaret from outside the main thoroughfare joined, we would play 'Cowboys and Indians'.

Summertime was the best time in the village, because - as we grew older – we were able to help on the farm and collect apples the likes of which you could never find today, and I can salivate over the mere idea of the fruit. The village hall (a large wooden Nissen hut) would come alive at this time of year with fruit and vegetable shows, flower displays and pie-making. Then, of course, we kids would get to dress up. On Saturday nights, dances would be held, and everyone would go, even babies and 'old people'.

Leighton even entered its young girls into a beauty competition and May Woodhouse won it. She lived in one of the chocolate box houses facing the park. She was crowned 'Miss Leighton' and went forward to the 'Miss World' competition.

Did I mention the pub? This did a roaring trade. It was more modern, and it had hanging baskets and a few wooden tables and seats outside.

The reason for its popularity was that it was situated in a lovely part of the village - opposite the village pond. This picture adorned postcards sold throughout Shropshire. The post office, village pump and row of thatched houses were also on photographers' lists. So, no wonder the pub did well!

Yes, Leighton was such a beautiful part of Shropshire and such a paradise for us children from the 'Dark Satanic Mill' town of Rochdale.

The Alchemical Magician

by Howard Gee

Jethro looked out from his farmhouse window at his bare fields which should have been full of his harvesting crops instead of the earth being dry and cracked. A tear rolled down his cheek. He had his wife and three children to feed and look after, and he had promised them that this year they would all have some new clothes and school shoes for the two girls who attended the village school. Jethro junior could wait a while for new short trousers but he did need desperately an extra blanket on his bed at night. His wife, Lizzie, never complained but he knew by her coughing throughout the night that she wasn't keeping too well and desperately needed a break from her heavy workload of chores.   He had been counting on a good harvest to help them through the year.

"I'm just going off to the bottom field to have a look", he shouted to Lizzie in the barn, "won't be long."

"Right", she shouted back. "I've finished milking Daisy and have just started on Gertrude."

As he made his way down to the field, his head was spinning; he just didn't know how he was going to feed and clothe his family. He was worried sick about their needs. His spirits were low and a sinking feeling was forming in his stomach. He bent down to examine the thick hard dry crust of the field and shook his head in despair. He stood up and was about to kick a stone in sheer anger when a slight movement caught his eye. He crouched to look around but couldn't see anything and was about to stretch his legs and walk away, when he heard a tiny whimper. He bent down again, moved a large stone and from under it, picked up a tiny grey field mouse. "What's wrong, little feller?" he asked.

The mouse seemed to look up at him and then down at his

front paw which had blood oozing from it and was obviously broken.

"All right", he said, "I have three little children who will look after you and get you healed before we put you back in the field."

Lizzie wasn't too happy about having Wattie, which is what the children decided to call him, around the house but like the rest of the family, she loved all animals and decided to help the children wash his wound, wrap a bandage around a tiny splint on his paw, make him a warm bed of straw and give him some heated milk, a bit of cheese and some newly made farmhouse bread to nibble on. After a couple of days, Lizzie encouraged the children to take Wattie back to the field where his own family would probably be looking for him, she told them.

Jethro continued with his farming chores, but he worried more and more about the drought and lack of any crops growing in his field. At last, he decided to go and see a man who lived in a cottage not too far away, deep inside a conifer wood. He was a bit of a recluse and didn't encourage folks to visit him, but it was said around the village that on occasions he had helped people in their hours of need. He had a special knowledge of minerals extracted from the earth, and the story goes that sometimes he could turn these minerals into gold.

Jethro was about to knock on the door when an old man with a warm welcoming smile, long grey hair stretching down to his shoulders and wearing what looked like a deep purple dressing gown with gold stars all over it, opened the door and said: "Come in; I've been looking forward to meeting you."

"Come away in", squawked a jackdaw sitting on his shoulder as the old man turned and shuffled back inside the cottage door.

"Oh!" said Jethro, "thank you." He stooped under the lintel of the door and stepped inside. "How did you know that I was coming to see you?"

"He knows everything", piped up the jackdaw.

"I can speak for myself, thank you", replied the old man. "My name is Wilfred and my little friend told me how you saved his life", he said, pointing to a little grey mouse sitting on the end of the table.

"He looks like Wattie", Jethro said.

"As you called him", said Wilfred. "He is one of my best friends in all the world and a few days ago, he was in the front garden when a large bird swooped down, picked him up and flew off with him, but - fortunately - as he flew over a dried-up field some distance away, he let him fall from his clutches."

"It was one of those obnoxious buzzards from the crags over the hill", croaked the jackdaw. "If I could get hold of him, I'd wring his scrawny neck and what's more …"

"All right, all right, calm down, Squawker", interrupted Wilfred, "our friend Pip alias Wattie was saved and is now in good health. When he landed on the hard ground, he rolled under a stone and the rest is history. You, Jethro, and your family saved my dear friend."

"How did he get back home?" asked Jethro.

"I sent Ollie, my wise old owl, out to look for him and with his night vision, he found and picked up our little patient huddled beside the hedge of the same field and brought him home."

Jethro looked at Wattie who held up his bandaged paw, smiled and in a squeaky voice said: "It was my lucky day and thank you so very much."

Jethro blinked in amazement. "We were indeed honoured to have you as our guest", he replied.

"How can I repay you and your family?" asked Wilfred.

"Well", said Jethro, "I really wanted some advice about getting crops to grow on my land again."

The old man paused and thought for a moment.

"I think that your bottom field is your largest one", he said, stroking his long beard with his gnarled fingers. "When you go down there tomorrow, I'm sure you will find a surprise waiting for you, and about this time every year as long as your family live and keep the field, my gift will be there for you."

After saying 'good-bye' and 'thank you', Jethro went home and the following morning, he and the whole family ran down to the bottom field. On reaching the gate they stopped, stood back and stared: the whole field was filled with ears of golden barley waving in the morning breeze.

A few days later, Jethro - full of the joys of life - went back to thank Wilfred, but he found that the cottage was in ruins and overgrown with trees and bushes. Jethro was never sure what had happened nor did he understand magic, but each year as he harvested his golden crop, he gave silent thanks to a very special old man.

Snow in early Fall

Travelogue - Part 1
by Monika E. Mackenzie

My fascination with New England has always been threefold: its history and way of life, the literature in all its forms about this part of America and the breath-taking autumn colours combined with white clapboard houses and churches.

The trip I made was a dream come true. My love of foreign places was nothing new, but the decision to finally go was triggered off by more than mere wanderlust. In the Spring term of that year, my senior pupils had been studying 'The Crucible' by Arthur Miller, set in Massachusetts, and recently, I had been reading Irving Stone's book about John Adams (who would become the second president of the United States after George Washington) and his wife Abigail, describing their early married life in Boston. Furthermore, since my favourite season of the year had always been autumn, I very much wanted to experience the legendary beauty of a New England Fall. I made the snap decision to fly to Boston in October of that year after I came across an Iceland Air promotion in the Scotsman sometime in July - £99 return and no mistake! It was a sign, quite clearly!!

Two-and-a-half months of feverish planning ensued and one fine day at the start of the October break, I found myself in John Adams country, literally. Boston was all I had imagined it to be as I walked from the subway through broad streets flanked by brownstone houses with autumnal displays of corn dolls, maize fronds and bright-orange pumpkins by their front doors. Looking left and right to take in the traditional architecture, I made my way to the YWCA in Back Bay, where I had pre-booked a room. For lone women travelling in

America, YWCA hostels are the best places to stay, and they can be found in most major cities.

After a more than comfortable first night in this astonishingly grand hostel, complete with an extensive library containing a grand piano, spotless and highly glossed marble floors and a beautifully decorated interior in the traditional New England colours, I went in search of the dining room ... although in retrospect, 'elegant dining hall' would be a more suitable description. Apart from the multitude of coffee flavours on offer from the line of dispensing flasks on a long shelf at the far side of the room, I had certainly not expected the lavish breakfast buffet that could have put any 4-star hotel to shame. When I had reached the end of the long serving counter, I was confronted by the most enormous black man, who - smiling from ear to ear and sporting a mile-high chef's hat - was standing behind a large cauldron and waving a ladle about.

"Syrrrup, Ma'am?" he boomed, and before I could say 'Boston Tea Party', I found my plate of scrambled eggs, crispy bacon, pancake and Hash Browns covered in maple syrup, just like Walter Cunningham's in 'To Kill a Mockingbird', when he was having lunch at Scout and Jem Finch's house. Strangely enough, it was delicious. It certainly set me up for the day, Sunday, and my planned walk along the Freedom Trail, which was to last five hours.

Dressed in sturdy, thick-soled shoes, raincoat with warm lining, a woolly, totally inelegant hat and a small rucksack on my back, I was met by crisp fresh air, bright sunshine and the bluest sky I had seen for days when I stepped through the ornate portal of the hostel. It was early, the church bells were ringing and apart from church-goers few people were about. I turned left - northwards - as a matter of course in order to commence the walk along the red-brick line set into the sidewalks, which started at Boston Common and ended at Bunker

Hill in the North of the city.

That Sunday turned out to be memorable in all sorts of ways, but one or two occurrences keep cropping up in my mind's eye: the meeting with an old, rugged-looking man sitting at the corner of Park Street Church, the 3rd stage of the Freedom Trail, where in 1829 the first speech in condemnation of slavery was made. This down-and-out vagrant, perched on an old upturned red plastic bucket, was playing the violin and - as I recall - rather beautifully. As I bent down to place a dollar in the hat in front of him I noticed a small cardboard sign on the sidewalk beside him which said, in uneven shaky letters: 'Smile - it's the Law!' It touched me more than I realized at the time, because it kept coming back to me for the rest of the day. The other thing that left a lasting impression on me was stage 13 of the Trail - the Old North Church, which had played such an important part in American history in 1775, when Paul Revere used its steeple, on which he had hung lanterns, to warn his fellow revolutionaries of the imminent approach of the British troops - one lantern if by land, two if by sea!

The next day saw me on a train to Concord, Mass., which Henry James once called the 'biggest little place in America', because this small New England town had brought forth more literary greats than any other place in the US. I went to visit the homes-turned-museums of Louisa May Alcott, Ralph Waldo Emerson and Nathaniel Hawthorne as well as Thoreau's 'Walden Pond' and the Sleepy Hollow Cemetery, which is the final resting place of these literary greats. It was a strange sensation to stand in rooms where authors of favourite books and novels had done their work more than one or two centuries ago.

In the morning of my third day, I went to collect the hired car that was to take me northwards into New Hampshire and eventually, through Franconia Notch, to Vermont. I had planned to take a detour via the town of Methuen on the north banks of the Merrimack River, approximately 30 miles north of Boston. Soon, I was on Interstate Route 93 and my elation knew no bounds. I came to the turn-off for Methuen before I knew it, and I drove through the centre at a leisurely pace in order to say 'Hello' for a colleague of mine who had lived here for some time during her early childhood. Soon after, I re-joined the Interstate at the Northern edge of the town. The weather was brilliant - bright sunshine and not a cloud in the deep-blue sky. I couldn't stop thinking how lucky I was and sang all the way to Manchester through an area that was once the home of the Pennacook tribe of Native Americans. Every ten miles or so, I stopped the car in a lay-by to marvel at the overwhelming palette of Autumn colours blanketing the forests on either side of the highway, which became more dense the further north I drove. It wasn't long before I came to the intersection near Concord, New Hampshire, where I had to turn off for the Shaker village of Canterbury which I planned to visit. Before me stood a beautiful little white church with the customary New England steeple, surrounded by a vast park-like lawn area, an aspect that I had been coming across repeatedly once I found myself in New Hampshire. I soon found the turn-off and for about fifteen miles, I drove through groves of silver birches till I could glimpse, through their white trunks, a group of farm houses which turned out to be my destination.

While driving through these woods, I had been oblivious to the change in weather. I parked the car in the designated area and stood, taking my bearings. Looking upwards I realized that the sky had taken on a leaden hue and my heart sank. I was feeling a distinct chill in the air while examining the board of directions, before walking over to the Summer Kitchen for something to eat. Early afternoon and most of the cooked food finished, I opted for two hand pies filled with apple and a mug of hot cider with a cinnamon stick for a spoon. Unusual! The placemats were laminated maps of the village and I had no problems deciding where to go next. The white cottage where they made their own paper was right across the yard and what I saw there was astonishing and inspiring. I ended up buying several rolls of the most beautiful hand-crafted gift wrap, some of which I have till this day, after well-nigh twelve years. I moved from building to building via paths lined with white picket fences and young birches and enjoyed the traditional, pleasing Shaker architecture. I glanced at my watch sporadically and experienced a faint feeling of unease - it was only early afternoon, but the light quality had changed so drastically that I decided to leave after I had visited the Art House and book shop.

Clutching the bag with two books of time-honoured Shaker recipes for bread and country fare, I stepped outside half an hour later and suddenly stopped. A bird had dared to drop something ... right onto my nose. I looked upwards but saw no bird. Touching the tip of my nose I found that it was wet; then I looked at my finger - nothing! Maybe it was the first drop of rain that had been threatening for the last hour or so. I hadn't yet reached my car when I felt another drop on my face, and then another. I stretched out my hand to check I wasn't imagining things and what I then saw astonished me: it was a snowflake settling in my palm! What?? At the beginning of October?

By the time I had resumed my journey north it was snowing steadily, though not heavily. I was becoming a little concerned - I knew I still had a long way to go before I crossed the White Mountains into St. Johnsbury, Northern Vermont. I passed the turn-off for Lake Winnipesaukee and now kept looking out for the sign that would announce the approach to the Old Man of the Mountain - a rocky outcrop high up that had the shape of a Native American Chief's head. Soon, I passed the Squam Lake area, the location where 'On Golden Pond' had been filmed decades ago. The snow was beginning to get heavier and I had trouble seeing very far. It was difficult to read road signs and directions, and my hands gripping the steering wheel were ice-cold. I had already switched the headlights on twenty minutes before and was aware of deep forests flanking the highway on either side. If my calculations were correct, I should have been driving through the old Abenaki tribes' hunting grounds in New Hampshire's North. It was at Whitefield where I had to turn off. I stopped and got out of the car to get my bearings - if that was possible - and sank into more than ankle-deep snow. Now what?

I resumed my journey very slowly so I wouldn't miss the turning, but so far - nothing. It must have been after almost an hour when I became aware of an array of dim lights in the middle distance. An accident? As I approached I found I was joining a queue of vehicles and thought: 'I was right - looks like a pile-up is the cause for this go-slow.' Cars in front of me were inching forwards and it seemed like an eternity till I could finally move on. I could now see a small lit structure right ahead of me - a café maybe? At that moment, there was a shadow by my side and a knock on my window. I turned left and saw part of a uniform. Police? I wound down the window and asked what had happened.

"Nothing, Ma'am", he reassured me. "Can I see your passport, please?"

"My passport? What for, officer?"

"Where are you heading, Ma'am?" He didn't sound quite so friendly now.

"I am on my way to Stowe, Vermont", I told him. "I am turning off at Whitefield, you know." Inwardly shaking my head, I thought: 'Silly man!'

"Holy Catfish, Ma'am! You are at Beecher Falls. This is the Canadian Border!"

7 seconds ...

by John King

Tick ...
the mysteries of life unfold
as the Ghost of Time glowers upon the anticipation
of a 'brave new world'
Tock ...
clouds conceal the rainbow's gold
soaking silent seekers in showers beyond the branches
of the mighty oak unfurled
Tick ...
gladrag strangers dive untold depths
through blissful bowers but gone is the oyster
which held the pearl
Tock ...
there is nothing more to behold
simple solutions like hillside flowers were on display
for every boy and girl -
freewill surpasses the mould
destroying centuries in hours for on 'democratic' heads
we granted the world
Tick ...
destiny devoid of form, enticed to play a hand
for too many, so easy to taint -
cold calm follows the storm
deathly silence befalls a land even romantics
refuse to paint
Tock ...
the hill lies bare, the seeds of no use
the answers which were to be ours
the earth dies there, through greed and abuse
the wind caresses the last wilting flowers
Tick ...

A Snowflake Fell

by Howard Gee

Albert could see the sky was grey as he looked up and through the bars of his cell. He wished now that he hadn't signed on the dotted line. He should never have lied to the Army Recruiting Sergeant about his age. There was so much he had wanted to see and do in life, but now there was no time left; tomorrow he was going to die. He hoped that his mother would understand why he had left home without telling her the truth about where he was going.

Thinking back, he remembered being lined up in the trench with his regiment at dawn, waiting for the signal to go over the top and the attack to commence. His feet had been constantly cold in the freezing water lying on the thick mud at the bottom of the trench; morale among his comrades had been low. There had been a chill wind sweeping across the fields of France and the biting cold had been creeping under his battledress searching out the innermost parts of his body, causing a shiver to run down his spine. 'Am I afraid to die?' he now asked himself. 'Yes! Do I want to die? No!'

He was trying to find an inner strength; thinking of his regiment, his country; trying to stop the tears rolling down his cheeks again.

Like a huge enveloping cobweb, he remembered, fear was quietly spreading and touching the very souls of the men who were engrossed with their innermost thoughts, waiting for the signal. Officers and sergeants were continually moving up and down the lines talking to their platoons, trying to raise their spirits in readiness for what was to come.

The barbed wire which stretched out in front of him looked so formidable and they knew that the enemy machine guns would be primed to rake the area in front of the trenches as soon as the first helmets appeared over the top. Silence and surprise were their best allies, the men had been told.

Down the line, the command came: "Check your helmet straps, rounds in the magazine, one up the spout and bayonets fixed, look straight ahead and when the whistle blows, do not hesitate - follow the man in front up the ladders and let's get the job done and be back in time for tea."

"Are you all right, son?" asked Smudger Smith, a senior member of the platoon who had befriended the young soldier since he had arrived from base camp behind the lines some months ago.

"I'm fine", he replied.

"Good lad", said Smudger. "When we go, don't hesitate, keep right behind me. I'll be your shield", he said jokingly.

"One minute to go!" The words were whispered down through the trenches. There was a deathly hush as the seconds passed. Silence! Not a sound to be heard, an eerie silence all around. More silence, broken only by the shrill of the whistles blowing loud, crisp and clear and as one, a synchronised movement of men holding their rifles with bayonets pointing to the front, went into action.

The front rank, already standing on the second rung of the ladder, went up and over the top of the trench led by the young Lieutenants and Non-Commissioned Officers shouting words of encouragement. The second rank followed and the enemy machine guns opened up. The noise of gunfire was deafening, smoke pervaded the dawn light, rounds penetrated flesh and men started falling to the ground, dead; stone-dead.

Just as Albert was stepping from the top of the ladder onto firm ground, Smudger Smith fell backwards on top of him, with blood gushing out of his head and from the front of his battledress jacket. Both of them fell backwards and sank into the beckoning coffin of mud at the bottom of the trench.

Albert couldn't move. His right arm was pinned under Smudger's back. No matter how hard he pushed, pulled and shoved with his left hand, he could not move. He had not been prepared for a dead body to fall back on top of him and he was struggling to regain his breath. He tried shouting, but his face was splattered with mud and his mouth and nose were full of muck and blood from Albert's wounds. There was no-one to hear his whimpers for help; they had all gone over the top to face the enemy.

Albert lay shivering and knew that his body was beginning to stiffen. He felt the rats crawling up his trouser leg and nibbling at his flesh. He jerked his leg and they were gone, but seconds later they were back. He closed his eyes and prepared himself to die; he was going to meet his Maker and would be ready when those icy fingers of death squeezed the life from his body.

He had no idea of time, but when he opened his eyes he couldn't believe that he was alive. He was lying on a hard wooden bench in a small room with a cold floor of earth and grit, but what shocked and frightened him most were the bars on the window.

A cruel, harsh voice was speaking to him: "Thought you could save yourself when you crawled under that soldier's body; thought no-one would notice; pretended to be wounded and didn't go over the top; didn't even see the enemy. You coward, you! Your comrades in your platoon, company and regiment died; you lived; but after your court martial you'll be shot dead."

The corporal left the plate of cold food and a tin mug full of water on the floor, spat into the corner of the cell, turned his back, walked out and slammed the door behind him. Darkness and fear swept over Albert as he closed his eyes and tried to take in what had just been said to him.

"It wasn't like that", Albert shouted, but it was too late. He could hear another door being slammed somewhere along a distant corridor.

At the court martial, Albert tried to explain what had happened, but in spite of swearing on the bible that he was telling only the truth, no-one appeared to believe him and he was sentenced to be shot for cowardice in the face of the enemy.

Time passed and one day, he was informed of the date that he was to leave this world and join his fallen comrades, including his old friend Smudger Smith.

On his last morning on this earth, a sergeant brought in breakfast of a sausage, a piece of bread, some beans and a mug of tea.

"Well, son", he said, "I don't approve of what you did, but may God forgive you and be with you in your hour of need."

"Thank you, sergeant. It didn't happen the way everyone thinks and I suppose I had hoped that I would be found innocent. I had thought someone would have believed me."

"There wasn't a chance that you would be found innocent", said the sergeant, "nor the other five who will face the firing squad, blindfolded and tied to the posts beside you. You will smell their fear and hear their sobbing, but you won't hear the shots fired."

Albert looked up and peered out through the bars, listening to the whistling of the icy wind outside and blew his warm breath into his cupped hands.

"I've put my extra shirt on so that no-one will see me shiver", he said. 'I don't want anyone to see that I'm afraid."

He was quiet for a moment, before turning to speak to the sergeant.

"I thought a snowflake fell past my window just now", he said. He took a deep breath and let out a long sigh, thinking of snowball fights and sledging in days gone by.

"At least you won't catch a cold, son; you haven't got time", the sergeant said quietly with a sense of army humour, but there was no laugh. "I have a son of my own, not much younger than you, and I look forward to the day when this war will be over and I'll be with my family again. The padre will be along to see you shortly." He stretched out his hand and touched Albert's shoulder.

"God bless you", he said, bowing his head as if in silent prayer, before leaving the cell and closing the door.

Once more, Albert was alone and his heavy breathing seemed

to echo around the dank cell, vibrating off the stone walls. He was shivering and frightened. He wanted to shout out, but nothing came out of his mouth; perhaps, he was too angry with the world and whoever had started this bloody war. He looked down at his feet and could again visualise those rats scurrying around. 'Much bigger now', he thought. He fell to his knees and wanted it all to end but was powerless to break free from his overwhelming despair.

A rattle of keys in the lock caused Albert to turn as the padre stooped and entered the dimly lit cell.

'I wouldn't have believed it', he murmured, brushing the snow from his coat and, without saying another word, laid his hands on Albert's arms and helped him to his feet.

"Well, Albert, how are you this morning?" he asked, taking his bible from under his arm and opening it up. "I have a message for you, and after I have read it, you might like to say a few words to your God."

Albert stood to attention, looked into the padre's eyes and whispered: "I'm ready, sir."

"Albert Macphee", the padre commenced, "you were found guilty of cowardice in the face of the enemy and on this day ..."

Albert's thoughts were drifting, drifting and he didn't hear the words being spoken. Outside, the snow was falling.

Albert shook his head, still in a daze: "Sorry, padre. What did you say?"

"You are free", said the padre. "A free man, Albert. You have been reprieved. You can go home."

"Home, sir? Free? But I am going to die."

"Albert, you are free and you are going to live."

"What about the others?" Albert asked.

"No", the padre said, "Only you. Your Commanding Officer always believed your story and has been supporting your innocence and fighting for your freedom these past months. He believed in you, but only God and you knew the truth."

"Do you think that I will be allowed to join my regiment again, sir?"

"Is that what you would like to do, Albert?"

"Yes, sir, and I would very much like to see my mother and all my family."

"In that case, I'll speak to your Colonel who, I'm sure, will be delighted to agree to the necessary arrangements."

The padre shook Albert's hand, wished him luck and left him to have a moment to himself.

"Thank you, sir. Thank you very much, sir", Albert called out. He knelt, bowed his head but couldn't control the tears. He remembered his comrades who had left the safety of the trenches only to die out there in 'no-man's land', where many were now stretched out in grotesque formations on the barbed wire, which had hooked into flesh and bone. His thoughts turned to those who even as he prayed were making ready to face death again in exchange for a free world. His thoughts turned to their families at home, waiting patiently for news and dreading the ringing of the bell by the telegram boy.

'Why can't people live in peace with each other?' he asked himself. He rose from the floor, easing his joints and again peered out at the falling snow. It was only when he reached for his army great coat that he realised it wasn't in his cell. He didn't care. He smiled and strode out through the open door.

Autumn

by Mary S. McLuskey

Mother sat looking at her four children and gave each a slightly dis-approving look. She had a knack of catching the eye of each child in such a way that each knew exactly why and what she disapproved of. Today was Autumn's turn; Mother clearly disapproved of her cloak. Autumn was the prettiest child with flaming red hair and skin as delicate as lace, and it often looked translucent. With eyes of brown and long willowy bones Autumn was indeed a beauty. She also loved to dress well and today, the 22nd of September, her birthday, she had selected her outfit as carefully as possible. Autumn knew she had until the 22nd of December before her brother Winter would have his birthday and be the one Mother would watch most carefully. Only three short months to make the most of her talents before one of her other siblings would take the reigns. It was this that Mother was concerned about; was Autumn ready to take the gift her Mother had prepared?

Autumn looked out the window to the kingdom below and blew a gentle breath out over the plains. A soft ochre touched the leaves in the trees and the air cooled slightly. She looked skywards and winked at her Aunt the Sun who shone brightly back by way of saying 'hello'. Autumn flicked her hair and a few auburn strands floated off on the gentle breeze to colour the foliage out over the heath. Mother kept a weather eye on Autumn as if to say go gently, and she did. She had learned a lesson from last year when with less experience she had too quickly turned the season and treated the land too harshly. The beauty of her palette had been lost to an eager brother who had waited in the wings, gently encouraging her to cool the air too much too soon so that he forced his hand upon her time and stole many of her precious days for him to play with in a winter wonderland of ice and snow. Not this year, though; this year Autumn was determined to hold off her brother's advances for as long as possible. If he wanted to fight with a sibling then she would let Spring take up the cudgel.

For the whole season, Autumn spent early mornings spinning wispy fog banks to roll down hills and moved over the land with her paint brushes loaded with colours of purple and red and yellow and brown. Her box of golden paints with their vibrant rainbow of colour belied the deadly secret held within. The fog banks may have brought with them soft dew drops of moisture for the plants and animals nestling below, but her painting told a story of retreat and decay. Around ten most days, Autumn would chat with her Aunt the Sun to ask whether today she would share a little of her warmth to heat the air and dissolve the foggy banks so that her decaying handiwork could be seen in a kaleidoscope of multicoloured hues. Each day Autumn would go out and bring with her more and more of her chilly tones, greedily plucking leaves from trees, withering branches and atrophying all things green as she passed them. As each day passed, her beauty, like the landscape, was ravaged by her efforts at play until her clothes took on a careworn look and her energy dissipated more quickly than she expected.

Spring and Summer had all this time sat with Mother, snuggled up with Winter who daily had edged a little further from the trio. He had watched with eyes that were cold and blue, waiting for Autumn to finally exhaust herself from playing with her cousins in the open plains and stripping the land bare, preparing the ground for him to take up the reins. As Autumn advanced across Mother's playing fields, Spring and Summer looked small and insignificant, sitting on Mother's left side. Summer's golden hair looked dry and straw-like, while Spring's usually vibrant green eyes looked dull and sleepy. Winter meanwhile was growing in confidence and strength; of the siblings only he could look forward at this time and smile. Occasionally, he glanced at Mother as if to check the time, but she would shake her head and point towards the clock in the hall; Autumn still had many weeks of play left to her. Winter could only wait patiently for his Father to move apace as only Father knew how.

In October, Mother took a walk with Autumn to admire her third child's handiwork. She was impressed with the beauty that had been bestowed upon the land and had even donned a magnificent cape made from leaf litter by way of appreciation for her daughter's talents. Like most Mothers, Earth was full of admiration for her children and when it was their birthday she would give them a small gift. This year, Autumn had earned a special gift - one of freedom of choice. In years past, Mother would have informed Autumn that she needed to provide warmth and sunshine for the farmers to harvest their fields; she would have shown Autumn the best places for her to ripen berries and fruits and given her the wisdom to kick-start the growth of vegetables that would be needed seasons ahead. This year, Autumn's lessons were over and only she would choose to make the sun shine or the wind blow, she alone would determine whether she would be kind or cruel to her Mother's flora and fauna that inhabited the earthly world below. Autumn had the choice of which cousins to play with, which Aunt or Uncle to favour and what games she and they would play.

This gift - the gift of choice - was considered the most precious of all gifts. Autumn had known for some time that this would be her prize for this season. She understood that in the past when Mother had allowed her to make decisions these had always been countered by that wisdom only Mothers can carry and Autumn had learned many lessons at the seat of her Mother's table. Now an adult, she could be benevolent and kind or she could be cruel and harsh; she need only to choose. She could even choose to defy her Brother, ignore her Father and continue her ways until Spring or Summer forced their will upon her when finally she would be exhausted. Father would march on, moving time inexorably forward but she, Autumn, could force him to acknowledge that her power was to rally her cousins, creating a symphony of elemental forces to stave off her Brother's hungry and cold heart. If she chose she could force her Brother back from his birthright so that she could reign for longer than Father had intended; his own Sister and Brother, the Sun and the Moon, happy collaborators in his Daughter's triumph.

As Mother and Daughter walked, Autumn told her Mother of her choice. She said that Winter had been too harsh last year and that Mother's beautiful earth needed a softer hand to tend her. As her daughter, Autumn would reward her Mother's generosity with a gift of her own; she would stand up to Winter and make sure he was kinder. She had made a pact with the Wind and the Rain, she had spoken to the Sun and all agreed, Earth should have a quieter time to recuperate from the severity of Winter and Summer's past outings. The Wind promised not to blow too hard. The rain promised to fall only when needed and then only in the right places, and the Sun was delighted that she, too, could rest a little and promised that no fires would be started by her delinquent rays. Mother was delighted with the wisdom her daughter was showing and warned her that Father would take no notice as he plodded on and onwards towards the end of time. She reminded Autumn that it was in the nature of things for them to step up when it was considered their time. After all, what would Father be for if not keeping time in order. Order was his domain and he did not like it when things were in disarray, no matter the reason for it. Autumn needed to know that Father was likely to support his Son, Winter, in grasping control on his birthday, December 22nd.

Autumn remained calm and determined that when her time had come she would do everything possible to keep it that way. She knew Father was a stickler for having all things neat and tidy and he hated it when things were not completed on time, but she was so enjoying seeing the countryside turn from lush shades of green into her softer golden palette that she wanted to keep it this way for as long as possible. She also knew that her Brother Winter would try his best to sneak into favour with their Mother and so steal away her precious time. Around mid-November, Winter tried his first futile attempt at pushing Autumn away. He sent an icy blast of cold air across the whole country - and having invited Jack Frost to tea - had proceeded to ask him to stay over for a day or so. Autumn was furious and immediately called her Aunt, the Sun, and pleaded with her to turn her rays towards Jack to shoo him away. The Sun readily agreed, saying that Winter and Jack were just too early to be playing together. With Jack banished for a while, Autumn went out to see how the landscape was looking.

Missing?

by Mary Perry

Oh, how I'm missing him,
his hearty laugh
and mischievous grin.

He had a knack -
a special way
to lighten up
my dullest day.
He had no airs
and no real graces,
but his one-liners
put smiles on faces.

He was good
at put-downs, too.
Anyone like him?
There'll be gay few.

He was my soul mate
and my friend,
too young to die,
his life to end.

Yes, I'm missing him -
I miss his cuddles
and his hugs
and kissing him.

Waiting

by Mary S. McLuskey

A clock ticked gently reminding everyone in the room that time was moving forward. Hope was no match for the inevitable passing of time and the drawing near of the passing of information from one person to another. This information was not welcome and if she could be anywhere but here she would. She looked around the room, a dreary affair if ever there was one. The NHS may have some marvellous staff but their idea of waiting area décor left a lot to be desired. The bundle of glossy magazines lying on the little wooden table were all at least a year old, with curled up corners and a germ-ridden look about them that put you off even the quickest of peaks.

The two women who sat opposite looked stoic and tired; one had a hat on to cover her bare head, the other fidgeted with the rings on her fingers. Yellow and black signage told of hazards, x-ray equipment, chemicals and other nasty treatments lurking for those who waited patiently. She sat patiently, waiting to be called. Like the other women she had come alone. She looked up at each passer-by: a nurse, a janitor, a young mum with a small child in a buggy. No one's eyes met as if by seeing someone you might somehow catch their disease. Noises were muted and the grey of the little waiting area did nothing to lift the spirit. Beyond this space were two paths: one led to fresh air and freedom to live and take life on, the other to a dark place where pain and fear were the only nurses.

She heard her name and felt the pit of her stomach drop; the lower intestine cramped in a spasm of pain that swept over her leaving her feeling cold. Her name was called a second time and at this she managed to stand. A fat nurse, with a grin on her face that looked as if it had been painted on and whose uniform looked as if it might explode at any moment, came towards her. She moved forward and the nurse turned her hand around in a semipointing motion. They moved towards the door of the consulting room in silent unison. A rather odd-looking man sat at the end of a long bench that had stirrups suspended in the air so that from her viewpoint they looked like ridiculously large earrings dangling from his tiny head.

He looked up and smiled a sort of welcoming smile. She sat down and he began to explain the procedure, pointing several times at the TV screen protruding from the wall at the head of the bench. He showed her the equipment and let her smell the heat of the metal that would soon scorch her flesh. She sat on the bench and manoeuvred into position while he adjusted dials and put on latex gloves. He talked incessantly about what he was doing, what she should be able to see on the TV and how marvellous it was that she was awake while he operated. She looked at the screen and watched pink flesh turn black as it was pulled away by steel grips. She could smell the flesh as it cooked and she watched in a distracted sort of way while the doctor made the final few excisions.

In the new waiting area the orange juice she was given was far too sweet and the biscuit a little soft as if it had been in the air too long. No one here spoke and no one made eye contact either. Everyone looked distracted, lost in their own thoughts about how their bodies had let them down, wondering whether the odd-looking doctor who talked too much had saved their life. She left the half-eaten biscuit and juice cup on the table and got up. At the exit she didn't look back; she would not return here no matter what the outcome. She walked home, two miles of torture in a state of stupor. At her front door she almost collapsed but managed to get over the threshold. Her man half carried her to bed and laid her down, aware of her pain. He stroked her head and kissed her before she fell into a deep sleep. He nursed her for several days without comment. They knew there was a long battle ahead before either might feel free or safe again.

Ten years on, the all-clear was eventually provided on a little card that simply said she should make an appointment with her local

GP so that she could join the normal programme of screening tests. For ten years, she and her man had waited for the letter to give the all-clear. For ten years, they had hoped and for ten years, they had held their breath, each time the letter arrived before seeing the words that allowed another year of life.

A Smile Found Me

by Melissa Macdonald

Frozen in this vast lake of my own creation; still, very still.
Outstretched fingers only inches from the surface -
my surroundings continuing without me.
Footprints lingered a while,
then were covered in a fresh crisp layer, alone.
An eternal winter had enveloped me.
I could see but did not look: why should I?
It only taunted me ...
Warmth soon caressed, no longer safe.
My lake was melting.
Breath forced itself in, the bright sun stealing my numbness.
I wanted to stay, but tears thawed my cheeks, I couldn't linger.
A smile found me, and it had brought the sun.

the rose beyond the tulips ...

by John King

sing my song ...

in the Garden She shone
golden hair falling like ripples
upon the blue ocean
the grace of a soul-light presence
before me
eyes smiling aflame within me

trip lightly ...

through the flowers?

shhh ...

allow your self the flow of the sylvan carpet
glide the light-path to the rose beyond the tulips

beyond the river?

no thoughts ...

allow the self to be guided by the melody
and in your Silence seek Me

closing my eyes I embraced the beauty within
footsteps rustling petals and leaves
the breeze
like a whisper caressing my features -
toes tripping tiptoeing through tulips
the meandering river and beyond
to white sands
a rose and the ocean

I opened my eyes
to the vision within before me
Her song singing

I am the Rose - I am the Ocean

the flower my heart
I dove the depths of my soul-reflection

The Hidden

by Denise Macdonald

Women gleam
Upon her fingers
Dreams and lives
Twist, shine, weigh.
The way their words would
Press upon her mind.

Golden moments and
The depth of affection
Contained in a jewellery box

Flicker upon her fingers
Sparking memory
Of smiles, words and tones
Even on a rainy day
They shine.

Picnic

by Monika E. Mackenzie

The cold weather had finally arrived. It was a good time for cricketers, golfers and tennis players to resume play, then sit around the club tea table after a free Saturday afternoon well spent.

It was the festival of Dussehra, which was celebrated as Durga Puja in Bengal. The men were enjoying a rare two-day weekend and, therefore, very relaxed. Someone came up with the idea to have some sort of a picnic the next day, Sunday, and it was agreed to go up through the forest to the upper reaches of the Murti, a mighty stream during the monsoon. We were to go in two jeeps, share the food preparations and - as always - take a driver, just in case.

So, here we all were - six of us, three children and Tommy, our driver. The men had already settled themselves on the large jute rug we used for outings; John was lying on his back contemplating the sky, and Ashoke was opening up a pack of playing cards.

"Anyone for water?" Saral asked, and without waiting for an answer went to fetch the basket with bottles and tumblers. Although we had finally seen the back of the rains, it was still quite hot during the day, so the offer of a cool drink was most welcome. My eyes swept over the vast expanse - the river was shallow now, and here and there the riverbed offered nothing more than pools, not deep enough for fishing, but ideal for the children! Man-sized boulders strewn all over offered the perfect setting for playing Hide-and-Seek.

"Right, you lot. Time to build a fire!" Rajin was the practical one and took Manju, Christopher and Babli to go in search of driftwood.

"Here, take the basket!" I called after him. Soon, I could see the little ones darting here and there, waving sticks, dry roots and pieces of driftwood in the air. It didn't take them long to fill the basket and before long, we had a fire going. Aruna was busy with a huge pot of channa, squirting the juice of a lime over this traditional Indian picnic food. I loved chick-pea curry and the aroma made my mouth water. Aruna was from the Punjab, and her cooking skills were superb. Saral was a vegetarian, and her dhal cakes and puris pure angel food. Enough said! I had decided to make the dessert. Since two of our cows had new calves, we had plenty of milk to spare and I had, therefore, prepared an enormous bowl of kheer, the delicious Indian rice pudding flavoured with green cardamoms. There were also some of the juicy new-season oranges that had been carried down a few days ago from the Bhutan hills.

While we were getting the food organized, our husbands kept the little ones entertained by playing with Frisbees and by pretending to be very silly. We could hear shrieks of laughter!

"Isn't it wonderful to be able to get away and enjoy such a beautiful natural setting? Oh, I just love picnics!" Aruna's joyful outburst was met with whole-hearted approval.

"Did you have lots of picnics when you were posted up in Assam?" she then asked me.

"Oh, yes. We did have quite a few", I said.

When nothing else was forthcoming, both Saral and Aruna burst out simultaneously: "Well?? Aren't you going to tell us about them?"

I gave them that mysterious look they so often teased me about, and eventually I conceded: "Well, there are picnics, and then there are picnics!"

"We are hungry!" the children shouted and came running towards us. So, for the next half hour all that could be heard was the silence of people who enjoy their food. Tommy had taken his filled plate and chosen a spot a few yards away from us - something he always did. It was a caste thing, and everyone respected it. After a while, I placed some more puris and chapattis on a plate and asked little Chris to go over and offer them to him. He loved Tommy, not least because he was sometimes allowed to sit on his lap and 'help' drive the jeep.

With most of the food eaten and high praises doing the rounds, our men settled down to Bengali PT - their forty winks. We gathered the dishes and utensils together and went to the river's edge. Scooping up handfuls of sand we went about cleaning the now crusted pots, cheerfully chatting as we did so. For a while, we were oblivious to our surroundings. When we were ready to put the utensils into the baskets, Aruna suddenly exclaimed: "Where is my large dekchi, you know the one I brought the channa in?" Looking around in consternation, I spotted it a few seconds later and pointed down-river. Though there was little water in the river it was enough to carry Aruna's treasured possession down-stream at a leisurely pace. We watched it, bobbing up and down, bumping into smallish boulders in its path.

"We need to get it before it is half-way towards the Bay of Bengal", shouted Tommy from the shade of one of the huge boulders, having by now abandoned his lie-back. Simultaneously, he and I jumped up and ran along the sandy bank in a bid to overtake the stow-away pot. Aruna and Saral were cheering and clapping their hands behind us.

Tommy saw it before I did!

He stopped in his tracks, pot forgotten, and put out his left arm, beckoning me to do the same. 'What is it?' I wondered. He was pointing ahead towards a fallen tree trunk, its top lying in the water, and he put his index finger to his lips. My eyes followed his line of vision and what I saw took my breath away: there, behind the top branches of the fallen tree, not twenty yards from where we were standing, a movement ... two creamy, rounded ears ... !

I blinked. It couldn't be ... my eyes were obviously playing tricks on me!

Tommy was beckoning me to move backwards while doing the same, and then he stopped. The creamy ears had now moved upwards, and what we were looking at was the beautifully marked head of a tiger. Clearly, it had come to the river to drink.

'How wonderful!' I thought. I had longed for some time to see one and wished that I had my camera. When Tommy turned around and saw the blissfully wondrous expression on my face he grimaced: "Memsahib, this is dangerous! We need to get back to the jeeps quickly."

I could see the fear in his eyes. Why did he always have to spoil it?

My thoughts went back momentarily to an outing a while ago, when we had been on our way back from the monthly shopping trip to Siliguri Bazaar. After crossing Coronation Bridge and driving along the pukka road through the adjacent forest, we had been stopped by a sizeable family of elephants approaching the road fifty yards ahead. In the lead had been a large matriarch, followed by several mature females with two babies in their midst, and bringing up the rear some youngsters and the most enormous Tusker I had ever laid eyes on. I had been ecstatic with excitement and urged Tommy to move forward so that I could have a closer look. He had been shaking like Aspen and told me: "Hattis are dangerous when angered. We have to get out of here fast!"... and with screeching gears, the jeep had reversed at a rate of knots. What I had seen then, facing us, was the Tusker - very angry now, with ears flapping and warning grunts emitting from his chest - moving in our direction.

I was roused from my brief reverie by jeep engines behind me. Saral and Aruna had obviously alerted the snoozing men and it appeared that time was of the essence. At that moment, I felt Tommy's touch on my forearm: "Look!"

The tiger was in full view now - a female, her teats fairly pronounced.

'Cubs!' I thought. We were definitely in danger! A quick sweep around the area towards the thick stand of trees confirmed what Tommy had been trying to tell me: two beautiful, very young cubs were ambling towards their mum - time for our exit! We found ourselves in the ready-to-go jeeps before we could say 'Bengal White Tiger'!

Leaning out to make sure the second jeep was following us, I let my eyes sweep over the area for one last look at the tigers and saw them – a cub on either side of the mother - looking at us quite peacefully. Behind us, about to get into the other jeep, I saw Tommy with his arms waving wildly in the tigers' direction.

'What on earth ... ?' I thought, and then ... a shout, and they were gone! My heart sank. What did he have to do that for? Aruna must have sensed my dejection and leaned towards me: "What's the matter?"

"He is such a spoil sport, isn't he?" I said, pointing behind us. She patted my hand: "We are lucky to be safe, don't you think? Tommy was just looking out for us."

"Although we have had a lucky escape", Rajin joined in - he had obviously overheard us - "we should also realize our good fortune. White tigers are very rare in these parts, and seeing one is good luck."

"Don't talk bunk, Rajin", Saral said. "Just concentrate on not driving us into a ditch!" Everyone burst out laughing, clearly relieved. When we had almost reached the fork in the road near our estate, I suggested that we should all go to our bungalow for tea. Since Rajin's jeep was in front, he indicated before turning off and the others followed automatically.

Several pots of tea, a huge plate of Samosas and a fruitcake later, everyone was very relaxed, lounging in easy chairs. The men were on the verandah, smoking and talking about seasonal issues on their respective plantations.

"How are we going to get our things back?" Aruna sounded concerned. Because we had been in such a hurry to get away, all our stuff had been left behind.

When Saral suggested that the driver could go back for it in the morning, I shook my head: "Uh, uh. There'll be no chance of that. He was terrified. Besides, if anything were to happen to him ..."

After a while I said: "John will take care of it! A shame we had to cut today's picnic short, though. We need to plan another one soon!"

Aruna and Saral looked at each other in disbelief: "You are joking, aren't you? I don't think I'll be going on another anytime soon!" Aruna sounded adamant.

"Come on, Aruna, nothing happened", I said.

"Would you listen to her, Saral? She calls 'being in danger of being mauled by a tiger' nothing!"

Saral laughed: "Well, nothing did happen." She then turned towards me and with that characteristic twinkle in her eye said: "I just remembered. Weren't you going to tell us about your picnics?"

Seeing that there was no getting away from it I rang for Nandu to bring that treasured bottle of sherry. When he returned with the tray he asked how many there would be for khana.

"Tell cook - six, and kedgeree for the children", I answered. To the ladies I said: "We might as well end this Puja weekend by eating dinner together", which delighted everyone.

We tip-toed towards the play-room to check on the children and admired the imaginative drawings of their fun-filled day by the river, before settling on the giant floor cushions in the sitting-room. I then poured three glasses of Sherry and began telling my friends about an adventure two years previously the details of which made our experience that afternoon look like a picnic.

Thunder

by Faith Pentland

The sound of darkness approaches;
Birds silenced by the sense of what is to come.

As the first droplets of rain connect with the ground,
The smell of warm, wet tar fills the air.

Brilliant light rips through the sky's shield then;
Nothing but the heavy sound of rain,
Absorbed by the thirsty ground.

Arthropods rush for their lives
To take cover under a canopy of leaves,
Animals scan their surroundings for shelter
from the sky's looming fury.

The angry sky erupts a deafening sound; nature has spoken,
Terrifying all in its path.
When will it end, this cycle of raging elements?

At last, calm.
The sky emerges from behind its deathly cloak.
The sun radiates life back onto the cautious planet.

A single bird call breaks the silence; normality slowly resumes.
But, as one life thrives, another steps into eternal darkness:
A bird's idea of heaven, and a worm's eternal doom.

One Fine Day

by Mary Perry

I stepped from the door this morning,
full of the joys of Spring.
Although there was frost-filled fog earlier,
I am sure I heard lots of birds sing,
and there was light now.
Blue skies could be seen all around,
Cotton wool clouds were sunbathing
and not one dark cloud could be found.

On crossing the bridge, the burn caught my eye -
it was no longer in spate, just babbling by.
I could see the stones 'neath the water so smooth
and dappled by sunlight - they seemed to approve.

I walked further on with a happier spring,
eager to find what the next views would bring.
I passed by some houses with very neat hedges -
they were covered with frost, and so were the ledges.

Menstrie Wood was a place with a possible yield,
showing some hints of springtime, and so was the field.
In the farmland on the other side
there were sheep grazing there,
making a change from the hedgerows
still empty and bare.

Approaching Blairlogie things weren't so quiet.
Starlings in the bare trees were creating a riot,
then joy upon joy I averted my gaze
and saw three young deer come down to graze.

Although spotting young deer was really exciting,
the activity on my side was just as inviting:
there were two squirrels bustling
through crackling leaves rustling,
their scatterings making vistas of beauty and awe.
There were flowers like tiny white bonnets,
fit to pen a few sonnets
about swans or these snowdrops,
which only Monet could draw.

Missing

by Mary S. McLuskey

Tom slowly unscrewed the bolts holding the panel in place and gently manoeuvred the cover so that it slid to one side, revealing a mass of wires and blinking lights. His hands were clammy, making the process difficult, and he could hear his breathing was elevated and his heart felt as if it might punch through his chest wall the rate it was pounding. There was no going back now, even if he wanted to.

Sarah watched Tom on the monitor, safe in the knowledge that he was oblivious to her observations. The cameras she had placed in the housing were so small that it was almost impossible to believe that they could produce such high quality images: they were also so small that detection was highly unlikely. When Tom slid the panel off, Sarah actually placed her hand over her mouth to stifle a gasp, even though she knew he would not be able to hear any sounds she might make.

Gabriel was fascinated. He sat at his desk, logged on to his personal security system and watched Sarah watching Tom. It was a curious little tableau that played out before him. Tom was clearly a very bad boy and messing with circuitry that he shouldn't even have access to. Sarah was just plain sneaky, using technology that Gabriel was impressed by even if he was concerned that Sarah's level of competence had previously been unknown to him. Not to worry - he'd recruit Sarah later; right now it was Tom's unsavoury behaviour he needed to keep an eye on.

Tom gently lifted a bundle of wires and put something inside the housing. Gabriel couldn't see what it was, but he would investigate that later. For now, he wanted to see what Tom and Sarah would do next. Unexpectedly, instead of leaving the scene of his crime, Tom moved to the wall and raised his elbow to the small fire alarm and smashed it, setting off the high-pitched building-wide alarm. Sarah's screen almost immediately went blank, telling Gabriel that she was definitely in the same building as Tom. The worm Gabriel had set off to locate her had sent an e-mail only a fraction of a second after the fire alarm, confirming what he already knew: same building, fourth floor, room number forty-two.

Sarah swore under her breath as she logged off her computer. She rolled over onto her back and smiled at the crude use of a worm to try to locate her. She hoped Gabriel, the head of security, was watching just as she had planned. It was so funny really, Tom and Gabriel doing her bidding without her even having to ask them. While Tom thought he was about to cause chaos using magnets to blow the computer and Gabriel was uncovering a major security breach, she was quietly reallocating funds into her untraceable offshore accounts. The Sarah known to her work colleagues was happily stealing millions of pounds without leaving the comfort of her bedroom.

As people emptied from the building, Gabriel rallied his troops. He implemented his security-breach plan and sent one team to where Tom and the source of the 'fire' was, while his other team headed to the fourth floor to apprehend Sarah. It didn't take long for both teams to realise that, just like the fire, Tom and Sarah were nowhere to be seen. Reporting this back to Gabriel had the effect of making him sit down and scratch his chin, temporarily unsure of what to do next.

Sarah stepped out of the shower and wiped the steam from the big mirror above the hand basin. She admired her blonde hair, glad that she had at last lost the mousy brown she'd had to endure for the past three years while she set her plan in motion. She began to dress in her new clothes - a small concession necessary to the next step in her plan. Checking her passport and picking up her hand luggage, Sarah headed for the door and the nearest bus stop, but not before setting light to the small caravan that had been her home for what seemed like an eternity.

Tom, too, was packed and ready to go and he expected to meet Sarah for their flight to Rio. Unfortunately, though, Tom was to be disappointed. Sarah was on her way to Southampton and to a month-long cruise once she had done a little shopping with her new funds. Tom was heading straight to jail if he was lucky; if he wasn't, Sarah would know that her other little surprise had kicked in. For now, Tom waited in the departure lounge of Gatwick airport, feeling a little hot and slightly concerned about the growing pain he had in his stomach.

Gabriel had now implemented his emergency plan and had called the whole management team into the office, having first had to explain to the fire brigade that the alarm was a fault. Two hours of trying to explain the situation to the management team had left everyone more than a little exasperated. Everyone had put into place their individual roles and checks so that they could report any issues and agree a way forward. The way forward for most was to get back to work and forget the whole miserable experience, once the police had been told about the apparent breaches in security and hopefully located the two missing employees.

A rather hot and sweaty Tom was stopped at passport control and asked to step into a small office where he was invited to explain his sudden absence from work, false fire-alarm raising and the business with magnets in the computer room. Unfortunately, before Tom could begin to formulate a response, he keeled over and dropped dead. Sarah would be quite proud of her handiwork, though she would never actually see the results; at best, there might be something on the news. A few days before she and Tom had shared coffee in the work's canteen, she had given him a slice of birthday cake and he'd gobbled it down enthusiastically while revelling in the fact that for once in his life he had a girl taking an interest in him. Sarah's only concern was that the poison she had put in the cake wouldn't act too soon and that poor old Tom would die before he actually put the magnets in the computer. Poor bugger hadn't a clue; all she had done was play a game of fantasy with him and make a few harmless suggestions; his own fragile ego had done the rest.

Sarah had paid cash for her tickets so that no trace could be made - unlike Tom, who had gleefully paid for their holiday with his credit card in the false hope that this was going to be their launch pad into a new life together. Amazing how easy it was to fool people! Even the name Sarah was just a slight change to her real Sara - just add an 'h' and you were a different person. No matter - Sarah/Sara was happily waving to no-one in particular as the liner left the dock. She joined with the other passengers in the celebrations as the ship slowly took her one step closer to heaven.

The police officer sat opposite the Chief Executive Officer and noted down a few facts as the latter embarrassingly relayed the details of the theft. Over 8 million pounds was missing from the company accounts and two employees also appeared to be misplaced. The police officer briefly thought about the post-mortem he had just attended and the report he had read the day before about a small caravan that had been burned to the ground by persons unknown. He wondered if there was a connection but dismissed the idea as a little far-fetched. With one person accounted for, albeit in unusual circum-stances, the police officer explained that they would, of course, try to trace Sarah Miles to ensure she was not involved in the robbery, but with so little information about her it would be difficult. He went on to explain that the address she had provided for personnel didn't exist and her bank account showed that she had never drawn on any of her wages paid into the account. It seemed that Miss Miles had another source of income and while she was missing, there was not much hope of recovering either her or the 8 million missing funds.

Mountainous Wonder

by Faith Pentland

Heaving muscles hold their pose
Eternally, never tiring, never straining.
A conqueror of our planet.
A mighty warrior.

To respect is wise
Or pay the price.
The mountainous masses, motionless,
Passively in control.

The constant flux of elements conspire;
Devastation in its grasp.
Wonderment never ceasing.

A most glorious feat of nature
Majestically dominates the land.

Love Words

by Mary S. McLuskey

What words of love do I have for you?
Which will I choose to touch your heart?
What form will I give them for best impact?
Oh, a dilemma so hard indeed.
Because you are so very dear to me
This love makes it hard to clearly see
And when I look into your eyes
The gift you give me does crystallize.
Your strength, your power and soft embrace
All make me know that in our human race
There is but one for me and he is you.
My darling Steve, you stole my heart
And I am sure you won't give it back.

Enemy of State

by Monika E. Mackenzie

In the small hours, one night in early winter, they'd come for him. The familiar clicking of the garden gate, the menace of their crunching boots on the pebbled ground and the abrupt demand at the front-door had told Elisabeth that life would never be the same.

And he had gone - so she remembered - with no resistance, a long, warm glance in her direction. She'd closed her eyes in silent confirmation of his plea. She'd long feared the day would come when he'd be taken and when she, if need arose, must wear his shoes. What was his crime, though? While he had known that what he was doing was right, he had also been aware of the risks involved. He had, nonetheless, felt secure in the knowledge that he had his friend's, the village mayor's, silent approval.

"Two weeks or more had passed", she told me, "when on my way to Church the mayor's son was crossing the village square in my direction, a self-satisfied smile on his face. His tunic, I observed, bore added stripes, which told the world - and me - of his 'well-earned' promotion."

It wasn't till the spring, she quietly recalled, that she had learned of the location they had moved him to: a camp deep in Bohemia, a Centre of Correction for Enemies of State.

"I never had my father's stoicism", she told me then, "and I often wept bitter tears for those who hid from persecution and the threat of death in the cellar rooms below my own, until the nearest moonless night, when they would be taken to safety under cover of darkness."

There would follow many days of trepidation until Herr Franz, her father's 'partner in crime', came after dark to say that all was well! And she, she'd missed them, all of them, each time some went to safety - like Ruth, a gentle girl and kind, and radiant Esther, then Joss and Hannah, that sweet young couple expecting their first child, and Miriam and Seth, the twins, whose parents had been transported east and were no more.

"It was the start of spring - two years or more since that dark day of his 'departure', when I heard the familiar footfall on the garden path", she said, remembering. "It stopped my breath!" She added that he'd filled the doorway as he'd always done, but now his hair was white. His death-pale face and laboured breath had spoken for themselves.

I learned that she had cared for him a month or more, through fevers, nightmares night and day, when - on a bright and sunny morning in Mid-May - she'd seen the change: the mouth's determination, the fire in his eyes! This only meant one thing: the tortures he'd endured had failed to break his spirit and resolve.

"And then ..." she said, her voice strangely quiet, "... I knew that his mind was made up! Not many days had passed when one morning, he told me of his plan. To beat Them at Their game, he said, he would join their party and sign on the dotted line, then follow his own heart to do what he must do - what he had always done."

Once upon a Time

by Denise Macdonald

"The problem is, he is charming", she whispered across the tea table. Her fairy godmother paused in pouring the tea, more than a little surprised. Magic leaked from her fingers and the teapot turned into a rather surprised white rabbit.

"He is charming? But he is supposed to be charming, that is his name, Prince Charming!" she replied.

"I know. But, you see, I meant to say, he is charming ALL the time!"

"Charming all the time? I would have thought you would be so busy arranging the wedding and becoming a princess - it was so very kind of the King and Queen to arrange that, and only two weeks to happily ever after - that you would not notice he was too charming."

"Yes well, that is another thing - then what?"

"Then, what?" Her fairy godmother peered over her pince-nez.

"I'm not sure that re-arranging all the shoes is really enough!"

"Shoes?"

"Yes. I get three new pairs every day. Most of them glass. It was very nice of you to give me the first pair. But, come with me a moment. Here!" Cinderella threw open a door with a flourish. Inside was a large white and gold room, and a crystal chandelier sparkled in the afternoon sunlight. The room was lined with shelves, each held up by a gilded plaster cherub. On each shelf was a red velvet cushion, and on each cushion a pair of shoes. They all had pointed toes and very high heels.

"All I do is change shoes and dresses all day!"

"And the prince? Have you spoken to him about this, about how you feel?"

"I hardly ever see him, I feel I hardly know him. We meet at the balls in the evenings; this week alone there has been the Moon ball, the Moth Ball and in honour of me the Foot Ball. During the day, he is out hunting or inspecting the guard."

The fairy godmother sighed. She had told the prince to marry Cinderella straight away. But there it seemed Royal Weddings took time to organise.

"Surely there is something else you could do?"

"No. See that mirror needs to be dusted; I could do it but, no - my job is to be decorative!"

Hearing this, the fairy godmother's heart sank. Something would have to be done. Just then, the Prince appeared. Even covered in mud he looked charming.

"Fell orff me horse. Never mind! Having a nice chat, m'dear? Good, good." He smiled at the fairy godmother, kissed the air somewhere near Cinderella's left ear and disappeared through another door.

"Charming!" said the fairy godmother. "Absolutely charming!" She frowned. Was it possible she had made a mistake? He had seemed so perfect. She gazed at Cinderella's downcast face. Perhaps, she needed something or someone else entirely?

Cinderella was walking in the garden, admiring the flowers and wondering if she could just run away for it seemed you really could not judge a prince by a dance, when something swooped down and grabbed her by the waist, lifting her high into the air. She screamed loudly as the palace disappeared far below her.

"Please don't struggle or I might drop you!" growled a deep voice. Horrified, she fainted. She opened her eyes to darkness and groaned at the presence of the several sharp rocks that had jabbed her awake. A large chain was wrapped around her waist and pinned to the wall. She stood and peered through the gloom. A light glinted ahead and she moved towards it slowly. The light winked out and then there were two, turned towards her - large green eyes shining through the dark. She tripped over something and the eyes came closer, peering at her. They belonged to a large dragon.

"Awake at last? You princesses can sleep!" he said.

"Why am I here?" she asked.

"Well, I am surprised - not a 'where am I'?"

"I can see where I am - a cave!" Cinderella stared at the grimy floor and traced a pattern in the dust with her toes. She had lost her shoes; it made her smile.

"Aren't you afraid I will eat you?" the dragon asked.

"No, I have a fairy godmother."

"So do I", said the dragon bitterly, "I am doing her a favour right now", he rumbled.

"Oh?" asked Cinderella.

"Yes!"

"I see", said Cinderella slowly, "I'm cold. Could you take these chains off?"

"No, you would just run away."

"I could give you my word I wouldn't", she said softly.

"Your word? What is that worth?" the dragon sneered.

"Oh, very good", said Cinderella, "do you practise that expression in a mirror?"

The dragon snorted and flames illuminated the very dirty and dusty cave. It also illuminated several skulls and bones.

"Oh my!" said Cinderella.

"Exactly!" huffed the dragon.

"Don't you ever do any housework?"

"Housework? Housework!" the dragon was astonished. "Dragons don't do housework. We terrorise people and burn swathes of countryside."

"Swathes? Not feet and inches, miles and miles or even kilometres?"

"Yes, swathes! There is a proper form for these things. You don't seem to know very much for a princess!"

"I'm not really a princess or, at least, not much of a princess."

"Really? You look like a princess."

Cinderella sat down in a puff of dust and sneezed. "I might look like one but I'm not. It is complicated."

"It always is. I have to go and cut a swathe. Tell me about it when I come back."

She watched the dragon launch upwards into the sky and then sighed heavily. She glanced around the cave; well, perhaps there was something she could do here? She tidied up and dusted and swept and then swept the bones into a pile. They made a strange noise. Curious, she bent down and picked one up. When she dropped it, it bounced. Rubber bones? Cautiously, she turned over a skull. Underneath, printed in neat letters, it said: 'Made in Hong Kong'. She sat down thoughtfully and waited for the dragon to return.

The dragon was impatiently pacing up and down outside the fairy godmother's house, at the back of a long queue, but he was shouting and finally got her attention. "Remind me why I am doing this?"

"Because you are a good boy most of the time", she replied, "and you needed cheering up."

"She is impossible, asked me about housework, and I believe she is not even afraid of me!"

"Oh?" the fairy godmother hid a smile. "Well, Prince Charming will be there soon to rescue her and you can have your cave back and go back to sulking!"

"I don't sulk! She might have screamed a bit when she woke up - it is unnatural! Are you sure this plan will work - the Prince coming to her rescue?"

"I am hopeful things will settle the way they should. Now back you go and remember - be scary!" The dragon rumbled a reply and headed home. He was surprised to see the torches lit and he gazed suspiciously at the heaps of dust. What had she been doing? Cinderella was sitting next to a cheerful fire, toasting some marshmallows she had found. He winced when he saw them; they had been in his stash along with … he groaned as she held up a magazine, smiling - 'DIY for Dragons in weekly parts'. "Marshmallow?" she asked.

"Look, you are supposed to be afraid of me; if you can't be afraid, the plan won't work", he huffed.

"Plan?" she stared at the dragon who was doing his best to look ferocious. The problem was she made him smile and he wanted to smile!

"What plan? Is my fairy godmother at the bottom of this?"

"Perhaps, Prince Charming should be here soon along with his guards to rescue you!"

"Rescue me? I don't want to be rescued, I'm having fun! And I don't think I ever want to see his Charming face ever again. I am not sure I am cut out to be a princess. I like people who do things, like cut swathes and stuff." Her voice got quieter as she realised what she was saying. "You have a fairy godmother? Are you under a spell?"

"Well, in a manner of speaking. If I meet the love of my life I might turn into a man; a terrible thought!"

"So you hide here in this cave?"

"It has worked so far. Do you have any more of those marshmallows?"

They spent the evening in conversation and then in stargazing. Cinderella curled up next to the dragon and fell asleep. He stared at her and then at the moon and fell asleep, too. He dreamed such a dream of a life with her and when he woke, it was to the shouts of the prince and his men. He stood up unsteadily. He was no longer a dragon; he could not protect her.

He shook her awake: "Look what has happened to me!" She smiled and threw her arms around him. Just then the fairy godmother and the prince arrived.

"I say", said Prince Charming, "unhand my princess, sir!"

"I don't think I will", said the dragon. He whispered something to Cinderella who nodded and then spoke to the fairy godmother who shook her head vehemently and then finally, reluctantly, agreed.

Instantly, the man was a dragon again and he scooped up Cinderella and flew up into the sky. There was nothing Prince Charming could do. He went home and gave up hunting and became a grumpier and rather more attractive prince. The fairy godmother returned to the ever increasing queue at her house and as for Cinderella and the dragon? They posted signs all around the cave that said: 'Please, don't rescue the Princess!' and they lived happily ever after ...

Winter's Revenge

by Mary Perry

When Winter saw January
Turned over its page,
He lost his temper
And flew into a rage.

"I'll show you not to end me
So soon in the year.
I'll visit the Arctic
And send back the fear
Of cold frosts and snow
To make hands and toes glow.

The die is cast -
There will be no more fun.
I'll nip fledgling crocuses
And blot out the sun.

I'll ice up the ponds
So that swans cannot land.
I'll send even more snow
Bringing cars to a stand.

This is what I call
Having my sweet revenge,
When snowdrifts are forming
From Perth to Stonehenge."

By February the 13th
Winter ran out of puff.
"I'm sorry", said he,
"I've done quite enough.

Tomorrow I'll just have
To swallow my pride
And ask February 14th
To be my sweet bride."

silent-life dreaming ...

by John King

the sage of the sun and moon
shines above me
in starlight and in song
and I listen to the melody to find
I am upon the road
of soul-dreaming.
footsteps
so silently treading.
have I danced this dream-song
upon ocean-tides
so long as to know
the road is within me?
have I sung the song of life
of the breathless whisper
of saints and angels
so long as to know
the road is before me?
have I spiralled the depths
of silent-life dreaming
for so long as to know
the road is me?
in dance and in song
the dance is I
as I am the dance of song.
lightfall-shoes
tripping lightly the way
on days of golden rays
and falling-light moonbeams.
is this my song?
I guess I am dreaming life
or so it seems.

Ode tae the Broom

by Mary Perry

It's guid tae be in Scotland
when the broom's so braw tae see.
The yellow o' the blossom
outdoes the sun quite easily.

It's no' the only blossom
tae put the sun tae shame
it is grown in fields commercially
under 'Oil Seed Rape' by name.

The crop, when ripe, is harvested
and ground to yield the oil,
which is put in plastic bottles
or made solid and packed in foil.

No such thing happens
to our lovely yellow Broom.
It appears just like an eclipse
between the sun and moon.

So when you trauchle doun the lane
and think your journey's all in vain,
you'll forget how dreich and sair the trek
when you spy that yellow Broom again!

A Moment in Time

by Howard Gee

Tommy was a southpaw. In boxing terms this meant that he led with his right hand as opposed to the orthodox style of leading with the left hand.

He had been attending the local boxing club in Edinburgh since he was fifteen years of age and had now, at the age of 18, entered the Scottish Amateur Championships. He was a strong favourite to win and be selected for the Scottish Team. Last year, he was a welter weight, but this year he had grown taller, his shoulders had broadened and he had put on a bit of natural weight and muscle on his biceps and around his diaphragm. He had now moved up to the Light Middle Weight Division, weighing in at 11stone 2 pounds.

He was an apprentice joiner, and his training involved roadwork and exercises in the early morning before going to work, and he was in the gymnasium almost every evening.

His training routine, which was strictly adhered to, involved getting up when the alarm went off at 5am, donning his tracksuit, trainers, gloves and woolly hat which were all required on cold mornings. When it was raining, he was often tempted to climb back into the warmth of his bed, but he knew that to win the championship he had to be fit. Running in hail, rain or shine was an imperative discipline, and run he did every morning. Throughout the run, he carried out warm-up exercises involving bending and stretching whilst carrying out shadow-boxing amongst the trees in the local park in conjunction with press-ups, abdominal exercises and step-ups, on and off the park benches, provided nobody was looking. His mother ensured that his diet included wholesome food with lots of nutrients - pastas, varieties of fruit, cereal bars and spinach. 'If it's good enough for Popeye,' she would say, 'it's good enough for my boy.' He drank lots of water and after work, there was always a healthy snack ready for him before he went off to the gym, and a welcome meal on the table after training.

He was dedicated to his training and determined to win; nothing was going to stop him.

In the gymnasium at night, he worked hard with his trainer on speed training, using the punch ball and skipping ropes in addition to ducking and weaving in front of the long mirrors that hung around the walls of the gymnasium. Co-ordination with his feet and hands was important, as was moving around the ring quickly, bobbing and weaving in the corners, using the ropes, following the trainer around, hitting punch-pads whenever they were held up high to assimilate left or right hooks to the side of the head or low to assimilate blows to the body. Being able to deliver jabs to the chin and straight punches to the target area were all required assets of a quality boxer, as was weight-training to strengthen the arms and legs. The evening always finished with sparring against the other lads in the club who varied in height, weight and style.

The coach would watch Tommy's every movement in defence or attack and at intervals, he would sit Tommy down on the stool in the corner and talk quietly to him. He would crouch in front of him and through various postures involving moving his head, with clenched fists waving in the air, he would demonstrate exactly how he expected Tommy to box. In addition, there were always the verbal coaching points before sending him back to the centre of the ring to try out his instructions against a new opponent. Tommy held on to every word of his coach and was a good student, enthusiastic and a quick learner.

The evening arrived, when all Tommy's preparation was to be put to the test. As the weigh-in was at 6pm, he was allowed off work early. It had been a good move to get a free ticket for his boss.

Tommy arrived early at the Assembly Rooms in George Street and weighed in on the scales with a pound to spare. He had plenty of time to see the layout of the hall, the ring itself, and to visit the toilet for the first of a number of nervous piddles before getting changed in the allocated red dressing-room. He changed into his shorts and boxing vest sporting the club badge, and before his coach wound the bandages around his hands which protected his knuckles, the red sash was placed around his waist and tied at the back. Once his boots were pulled on and laced up, he could start his loosening and warming-up exercises in the changing-room. With 15 minutes to go, the 8-ounce gloves were pulled over his bandaged hands and his dressing-gown slipped over his shoulders. His coach knew that Tommy would have butterflies in his stomach and spoke calmly and reassuringly to him while he waited for the current bout in the ring to finish. He placed Tommy's gum shield into his own tracksuit pocket, ensuring that he had it when they climbed into the ring.

The Master of Ceremonies called Tommy and his opponent into the ring and introduced them to the crowd. Tommy was in the red corner and his opponent in the blue, both wearing the coloured sashes accordingly.

Both boxers were called to the centre of the ring by the referee who told them to listen carefully to his instructions during the bout: "Stand back if told to do so and go to a neutral corner if I stop the bout for any reason", he said. "In the event of one or both of you slipping or being knocked down on to the canvas, you must listen to my count, stand up, wipe your gloves on your shorts and commence boxing on the command 'box'. Shake hands now, return to your corners and come out boxing when the bell rings - and let's have a good clean contest."

A few last words of encouragement were whispered in Tommy's ear by his coach, before he placed the gum shield into his mouth, smoothed a bit of protective vaseline over his eyebrows, wiped his brow with a sponge and left the ring as his assistant cleared the corner by pulling the stool under the ropes. The bell rang and Round 1 was underway.

Tommy's opponent was an experienced boxer and the scar where stitches had been inserted above his left eye was clearly visible. In spite of his stocky frame, he moved around the ring with ease. Both boxers were about the same height with similar arm reach, but twice Tommy was caught with a left hook; the second one had sent him reeling against the ropes and he had to adopt a defensive stance to cover up and jab his way out of trouble. The bell went and Tommy was glad to return to his corner and sit down on the stool. His coach removed the gum shield, dropped it into a beaker, gave him a sip of water, stretched out his legs, sponged and towelled him down, before telling him what he had to do in the next round. Returning his gum shield into his mouth, the coach assisted him off the stool and left the ring, stepping out between the ropes as he heard the call 'seconds out' and the ringing of the bell for the second round.

Tommy was down on points, because once or twice he was caught on the target area, allowing the judges to score accordingly, and when the bell went for the end of the second round, Tommy was again glad to sit down in his corner, be refreshed and listen to his coach: "You need a stoppage by the referee - unless you knock him out - because he is now too far ahead on points."

The bell rang for the third and last round and Tommy had three minutes to win the contest. Both boxers circled around each other, throwing a few feints, straight punches and jabs, parrying and blocking with gloves and elbows when suddenly, they were in a tight clinch in one of the corners, hugging and pulling each other in close.

"Break!" called the referee, and when both boxers stood back, Tommy realised that his opponent was breathing heavily, dropping his arms and tiring rapidly. The opportunity had arisen for Tommy to step forward, feint with a right to the body, bring a jab up to his opponent's jaw and follow through with a left-hand upper cut under his chin, which is exactly what he did. His opponent's knees buckled and - as he crashed to the floor - the back of his head hit the canvas with a dull thud and he was out cold. The experienced referee didn't even start the count and immediately waved the doctor into the ring.

Realising the seriousness of the situation, the cheering and jubilation - not only in Tommy's corner but throughout the hall - was smothered suddenly under a blanket of silence. Tommy watched as the doctor knelt over the unconscious boxer and signalled for an ambulance to be called. His opponent was carried out of the ring on a stretcher, which was slid underneath the bottom rope held up by the Master of Ceremonies.

Tommy stared on in disbelief. He would never forget that moment in time when his opponent's head hit the canvas. He had won the contest but decided not to go forward to the next round, and although his opponent did recover, Tommy never boxed again.

He now spent more time with his girlfriend and sometime later, he started learning Judo, the art of the gentle way.

Spiderman

by Monika E. Mackenzie

To learn of his decision to leave and go abroad again was like being hit in the face with a wet fish.

Jan had been so chuffed to finally have a flat of his own, and we, his family, were happy for him. Often, he spoke of the smell of the sea and the ships he saw skimming the horizon when out early, jogging past the new residential blocks at the shore that were, according to council officials, destined to sink. The open spaces, the close proximity of the sea and the view on hazy mornings across the Firth to Burntisland, which conjured up childhood memories ('but it looks grander from across the water', he had said), maintained his contentment, as did restful nights undisturbed by traffic.

The inner courtyard, tranquil with verdant hues and birdsong, confirmed to him the prudence of his choice. All was well; life was good.

It was like a bolt out of the blue, therefore, when - in late autumn - we received his news that he was going to leave the place. Incomprehension was replaced by consternation when eventually, a full explanation shed light on his unexpected decision: wide-open windows at night and being a light sleeper had caused him to become aware of sinister goings-on during three separate nights in one week.

At first, increasing unease that nudged him through his morphean awareness made him rise and stand by the open window, the crisp night air clearing his head instantly. The silvery half-moon light revealed the cause of his broken sleep: a dark figure scaling the house wall opposite, feet on a horizontal drain pipe. With bated breath he observed the acrobatic progress.

'What the hell?? This can't be happening!' he thought. The would-be intruder, now busying himself with a second-floor window left unsecured, demanded intervention.

"Hello, police?" Jan whispered, giving details.

"Has he actually broken into the house?"

"No, but..."

"In that case, sir, there's nothing we can do. I suggest you go back to bed!"

Back at the window, he now saw a light go on in the building opposite and a moment later, Spiderman swiftly clambering down a drain pipe before taking to his heels.

There was little thought of sleep for the remainder of that night.

Two nights later, he witnessed a similar occurrence, though earlier than before. He had been waiting in curious anticipation. From his darkened bedroom the mysterious figure could be seen spying through a lit window opposite - the curtains had not been drawn. On this occasion, two young constables eventually came - too late, of course. The intruder had been disturbed and run off.

About to leave, one of the uniforms said, with a patronizing pitch in his voice:

"Sir, if you don't mind my asking, what exactly is your reason for being up in the middle of the night, looking out of your window?

Was he for real??

"I'd have thought that was fairly obvious, Constable."

The two greenhorns left, giving him one of those 'we-know-your-type' looks.

Taking matters in his own hands, Jan visited the flat opposite after work next day. The couple, confirming that they, too, had phoned to report an intruder, had found the police's response equally ineffectual. Then, on Friday night, after having been out with colleagues and just about to drift off, he heard a sound, resembling the snapping of a branch. The night was wind-still and the moon almost full. He leaned out of his window, glimpsing the now familiar dark figure. Carrying something boxy, Spiderman was on his way to the gap in the slatted wooden fence.

The next morning, while buying provisions at the small grocery store down the road, the owner shared his upsetting experience of a break-in at his home the night before and the theft of his computer. Jan was taken aback momentarily, but then he simply asked:

"Where do you live?"

"Third Floor - 22, Fishers Lane", the man said.

'Bingo!!!' Jan thought. 'I saw your thief last night.'

After telling the man that they shared a courtyard, he described his nocturnal observations of that week and the police's concerted efforts in crime prevention. He then came to the conclusion that if Spiderman managed to get to the third floor and transport stolen goods down a wall, and since the local police were trying their hardest to impersonate the three wise monkeys, he would have no chance on the first floor, with a drainpipe half a yard from his window ledge.

A Moment in Time

by Faith Pentland

A second passes, a non-returnable moment in time;

Made, then dissolved in dimensions
Oblivious to Man.
Moments fleet,
Effortlessly merging into the next,
Never ceasing to exist;
Time has control.

In a moment, the world can change;
Nothing stays still.

Time, constantly in motion;
It never repeats.
Mystery surrounding timely wonders.
Existence, defined by a moment in time.

Labyrinths

by Denise Macdonald

He always watches her, waiting for something, staring over the heavily patterned silver, his eyes shining through the flickering candle flames. She was waiting, always waiting, and for what? Often they have guests; she is always gracious, as she has been taught. She is glad she cannot understand their words; their looks are enough.

Every evening, he asks for the keys and searches through the bundles that weigh her down through the day, as she wanders the labyrinth he calls his castle. There are so many doors and rooms. Above each door a face carved into the stone. A jester above this dining hall, where she watches them emptying their glasses and calling for more wine, more ale, more food and more music. They are always calling for more of everything.

The mute pity of the servants disturbs her; she knows they might tell her something but they are as afraid as she is, startling at shadows and the iron clang of their master's footfall. And so she escapes into her sewing - she is making him a fine shirt with a monogram. He was surprised when he saw it; for a moment she saw some pity in his face, but it was chased away by that smile that does not reach his eyes.

There is one door which always frightens her. It has the smallest lock and the sweetest silver key, the fob heart-shaped. Above the door, a black rose carved from obsidian. She remembers, ah … she remembers her grandmother's tales. Beneath the rose there are secrets to be told, to be kept, to be wary of. And yet, she is the mistress of this great castle and he claims the mistress of his heart. And she knows she is lucky to be married to such a knight - even with his coarse friends. Her marriage gave her family, wealth and land.

He is very generous; she has fine gowns and everything her heart could desire except true love and affection. She knows his mind is always turned towards the next tournament, for he has a reputation to maintain and the crowd to please as they wave the blue ribbons and chant his name - Blue Beard!

brown heather and wild

by John King

I am a soul adrift
sylvan haze mist-mountains -
brown heather and wild

dream wisp-clouds grace my gaze
in memory fading -
a child gathering rose petals
to release upon the breeze
lost in their mystery dance
swirling in eternity

innocent eyes
imbibe the beauty therein
and I pray she will stay

she smiles
offering herself to the sun and moon
as a gift in still-life ascending
but as I seek to reach her
she is gone

the light of the firmament
presents a white petal and I
united with the presence
hold her close
as a tear in memory and joy
falls
cleansing my heart
and I let her go to her home adrift
sylvan haze mist-mountains -
brown heather and wild

The Hidden

by Mary S. McLuskey

They were talked about in whispered tones, no-one ever mentioning their names or referring to them directly. Sometimes, they were called 'the hidden', but more often they were ignored in the hope that they would die or just go away. It seemed an age since anyone had actually seen them and rumours had recently started to circulate that they were responsible for the spate of missing persons. Speculation was rife and no matter how many times the town's folk called for calm, there was a small group who seemed determined to make trouble.

Hidden from sight for more years than they could remember, the family kept a weather eye on the people outside, knowing that they were feared and that fear was the thing that had kept them safe from harm for so long. The people on the outside didn't know if there were diseases or infections that they might catch if they were to come into contact with the family, and the family were happy not to disabuse the outsiders of their fears. They were not a pretty sight, with pock-marked skin and odd growths scattered over their bodies, but this was a genetic family problem, not something contagious.

A group of young men began to gather at the end of the dirt track. They were carrying batons and their voices were raised. One had a bottle with a rag flowing out of the top and he danced from foot to foot as if getting ready to make a dash. Others shouted over the noise, egging each other on and forcing those at the front of the group across the threshold between the track and the pathway that lead directly to the cottage's front door. From somewhere in the crowd a voice shouted:

"Scum! Go back home; leave us alone.'

Another voice shouted: "Get out, get out; go home, go home."

And another, more menacing voice could be heard to scream in the direction of the house:

"We're going to burn you out, if you don't go now!"

Behind the window in the front room the eldest boy stroked the gun he held in his hand and watched the gathering crowd as they played out their little game. Like so many times before, he watched as boys his own age played out their ritual. This time, however, there was a more sinister feel to the crowd's taunts. This time, there seemed to be more people than ever before and there were women now; that had never happened. Behind him, in the small room, his mother sat rocking in the chair beside the fireplace, her hands and face grotesquely deformed by the genetic fingerprint she carried. In her lap, a small bundle of a baby slept quietly, unaware of the storm gathering outside. She stroked the baby's smooth unblemished skin with a knotted finger and, hearing the shouts from outside, pulled the baby closer as if to protect it from harm.

A woman in the crowd laughed and pushed her way towards the front of the mob. She grabbed the rag- topped bottle from the gawky youth and brandished it in the air. As she did, the youth pulled out his Zippo lighter and set the rag aflame, laughing and dancing like a fool as he did. In slow motion, the woman watched the flames dancing up the petrol-soaked rag and beginning to lick around the top of the bottle neck. Muffled voices shouted to her:

"Throw it!" "Get rid of it! Quick!" "It's going to explode! Run!"

Terrified and confused, she launched the bottle high up in the air and in the direction of the cottage. It turned over, rotating like a pinwheel before it began its descent, exploding over the central dormer window, sending a cascade of flames and fuel across the roof top.

The door to the back of the house crashed backwards and forwards in the wind, banging like a drum to the rhythm of the crowd's shouts. Inside, yellow flames dropped like liquid gold to the floor and onto the rug at the fireplace. Tendrils shot out from each drop and flames danced over the floor and up the walls, engulfing everything they touched. A baby's toy seemed to melt while the flames crept around it before it exploded, sending out melted plastic to fuel an even more intense fire. Curtains that had been hand- stitched gave in easily to the fire, but the child's cot in the corner of the room smouldered for a long time before any flame appeared.

The woman who had thrown the petrol bomb had laughed with the crowd as they applauded her handiwork. Then, as she saw the flames take hold of the small cottage, she began to fear that what she had done was not such a good idea after all. She sank back into the crowd, looking for a way to leave this place, to leave behind her what she had become. The crowd shouted and screamed, mob-like, watching with glee as flames tore at the building, consuming everything in it and sending plumes of thick black smoke high up into the air.

A tear slipped down the mother's face while she watched her husband and son pull the cart that held all of their possessions through the unseen path that would lead them through the forest. She prayed that this time the road would be easy and that the family would find shelter that they could call home. Her baby slept, as before, unaware of the pain and sorrow around him. She looked at her husband's back as he pulled the weight of their world alongside his son; two sets of strong shoulders, two strong men to care for her and the child - but not enough to fight off this cruel world and this disfiguring gene! The air had the smell of tar and wood smoke and she tried to let go of the image of her front room with all its familiar things - the hand-carved table, the glass lamp her own mother had given her, the little wooden toys that the father had begun to carve for his newest son.

The woman broke away from the crowd and began to walk as quickly as she could in the opposite direction of the fire. She was unfamiliar with this part of the town - she never came here because of all the stories and tales about the hidden family. The light had almost completely gone and now with no flame to show her the way she soon was lost in the tangle of trees and bushes that surrounded her. She cried out, calling for help, but she was too far from the noisy crowd to be heard. Then, in the distance, she saw two men pulling a cart with what looked like bits of furniture stacked on top. There was a woman walking behind the cart and she seemed to be carrying a baby. Awash with relief, she rushed towards the little group, hoping to find salvation.

Mother turned in fright to see a woman rushing out of the trees headlong in her direction. She pulled the baby to her protectively and called out to her son. She need not have worried; his shot rang out as her own voice sailed through the air. The bullet's trajectory was short and fatal, bursting through the skin and bone of the woman's chest before piercing her heart. The sound of the single shot echoed across the forest, but the ferocity of the flames and the gaiety of the noisy mob deafened the world to its sound. They walked on a little more quickly than before, not daring to look back, not daring to rest.

Unrequited Love?

Molly saw Jack
and gazed with awe
as the men all made
fine stooks of straw.
She thought, as the men
used every sinew:
'Does your heart, my dear,
Beat fast within you?
For I want you to be
my Valentine,
when two hearts beat as one
for now and all time.
I'd come and join you
if only I could
but, alas, I am made
of new straw and wood.
The WRI competed
To make a straw dolly
I'm the first prize –
My name is Molly.'

The Journeyman's Destiny

by John King

he spoke of his birth
as the desert sandstorm

of dusts and mists and rains

eyes of seeing

teardrops
falling
rippling silent pools
of soul reflection

he spoke of his life
as the desert mystery

of soul-saints and angels
weaving
their golden thread
through desert petals
omniscient

of no beginning nor end

he spoke of his death
as the desert flame

of suns and moon and stars

the numinous beauty of love
illumined -
shining within

No Love, No Soul, No Life Thereafter

by Gary Smith

Did I break my soul while bones did heal?
Did I squander life and make a meal
of the joy beholden to each and all,
and curse my love with unearthly squall?

Is there time enough to cast this soul,
Sand enough to fill the hole,
Or should I just accept my fate,
exist inside my fortress, hate?

The will that lived, not forgotten
Though jackals carry the force begotten,
The life I give is poor and weary
But the message still is screamed out clearly ...

I watched as he did reanimate primal,
I cried as I did rush to final,
I screamed aloud, "This is all wrong!"
But I was proud and carried on.

Knowing now I am alone,
Might grind to dust the densest bone,
But somehow vigour does return
Behind dead eyes, inferno burns!

No myths nor legends do I need
For common sense alone does lead
Myself to spread as fire does
And wings to spread, for spread they must.

On this night and each thereafter,
The love of life, the sound of laughter,
Must be paused, postponed until,
My abandoned soul ... returned its will.

Ochil Writers' Group

Howard Gee was born and educated in Edinburgh and has worked, travelled and lived throughout Europe and the Far East with his family who are now all very happy to be living in the shadows of the Wallace Monument near Stirling and the magnificent Ochil Hills which are truly an inspiring background to encourage all who wish to write.

John King is a dreamer, a seeker, a soul-journeyman - a poet, an artist, a musician. It is his desire to share his journey and the beauty he has found.

Denise Macdonald loves words and language, the shape of words on a page, the curl of letters as they unfold through a story. She enjoys trying to make the words dance at the end of her pen! Her other passion is drawing and illustration; lost for words she will often reach for a drawing pencil to fill in the blanks.

Melissa Macdonald is a Theatre Technician based in both London and Central Scotland. She has a passion for writing poetry and short stories. Currently she is in the early stages of writing her first play.

Monika E. Mackenzie came to these shores more than thirty years ago. Fascinated by words since she held a slate at infant school in her native Germany, she has always enjoyed writing. Her life in India provided her with a wealth of ideas - many of them about encounters with animals. If she ever has the inclination to write her autobiography, she will probably call it 'A Life Less Ordinary'.

Mary S. McLuskey has been writing for many years and first published with Kogan Page in 1996. Since then Mary has won Best Adult Poem in Lomond Writers' 2012 competition. She has published several poems with Poet and Geek, Poetry Scotland and Federation of Writer's Website, February 2012.

Faith Pentland was born in Menstrie in 1978 and lived there until the age of eight years old. She returned ten years later after living in England. She gained an MA in Philosophical Studies at Glasgow University in 2003 and a Diploma in Health Care Studies at Cardiff University. Her main genre in writing is Poetry, which can be experienced through a number of different styles.

Mary Perry has lived in Menstrie village since 1962. Originally from Rochdale in Lancashire, she has had a lifelong love of poetry but only recently began to write for herself. The wrong side of seventy, Mary intends to keep on going.